SWAY

A MESSAGE OF
PERSEVERANCE AND FAITH

John Cicero

ISBN 978-1-0980-0218-3 (paperback)
ISBN 978-1-0980-0221-3 (hardcover)
ISBN 978-1-0980-0220-6 (digital)

Christian Faith Publishing, Inc.
832 Park Avenue
Meadville, PA 16335
www.christianfaithpublishing.com

Printed in the United States of America

Contents

Preface

S way initially began as a challenge from my cousin and dear friend, John Ryan, to attempt to write a story from an experience he had while moving down south for a new position in his company. John apparently was being attacked by a nuisance of a weed while cutting his grass in his new yard. The weed, uniquely, had a mind of its own and mysteriously could never be eradicated from his yard. The annoyance had gotten so bad it made an indelible impression mentally and physically on John which thoroughly convinced him a story could be created. Thus, the challenge began.

Fast forward a few years later and fueled by a few unsuccessful attempts to bring John's story to life, I found myself dealing with my own unique challenge of an undesirable weed. I found a tiny sunspot on my face near my right eye which migrated into melanoma. After four surgeries to remove this nuisance. I was now dealing with a hole in my face the size of a golf ball. A major surgery with a pretty intense recovery followed. Through this all, something triggered in me to write. The genesis of Johns' original weed story suddenly made more sense to me. I was uniquely motivated now more than ever and I had a new twist on the story I just had to craft.

This is when little Norah Petre, whom I have never met and was just eighteen months old at the time, entered my life. I am fortunate to work with Norah's father Marc, who saw me at a conference from a distance with my battered surgical face.

The following week I received an e-mail from Marc with a simple phrase in the subject line, which read, *Sway*. Not only did this catch my attention but the uniqueness of the phrase activated something in my heart I couldn't describe. Marc went on to tell me in the e-mail how he had been with his sweet little daughter on their porch over the weekend staring up at the trees when Norah blurted out the phrase. As she said '*Sway*', Marc looked up at the trees waving in the wind and said for some reason he thought of me. Needless to say, I was moved beyond belief and thoroughly convinced God had communicated to me indirectly through this sweet little girl of just eighteen months old. From that day forward, I had the title of my story and a unique direction for my new book.

Perseverance and undeniable faith in God. Wow, the theme of the story and quite frankly my life. After writing *Sway*, I thought I was done with our health dramas until the day I found out the love of my life had been diagnosed with pancreatic cancer just eight months after my final melanoma surgery. My wife, Debra, who embodies perseverance and faith would now have to go through her own journey of eradicating a nuisance of a weed.

If you know anything about pancreatic cancer it has a notorious and frustrating reputation. One so frustrating it tends to suck the very wind out of your sail even before you have to fight it.

Immediately, Debra's diagnosis prompted a recommendation to excise the tumor through what is known as the Whipple surgery. This surgery is not only intense but it is described as one of the most challenging surgeries next to open heart.

The night before her surgery Debra received a random e-mail from a friend of hers which depicted an image of a surgeon performing a surgery. In the image, next to the surgeon, stood Jesus guiding the surgeon's hands. It was a beautiful image that gave us all comfort the night before her surgery. Ironically, we came to realize the image was not only beautiful but it was amazingly true. During the surgery the surgeon nicked an artery and had to miraculously save Debra even before the Whipple procedure began. Needless to say, we were all convinced Jesus guided the surgeon hands that day and most definitely had our backs throughout this intense procedure.

As the weeks went on we were brought to our knees more than once when we were given a diagnosis of the worst type of pancreatic cancer. To compound this, the treatment prescribed was also the most aggressive type of chemo. Our family and friends rallied behind us like no other. This is when the power of prayer kicked in and the miracles intensified. Each week another milestone fell and the prayers strengthened. Some news was good and some bad. Through it all God remained a steadfast in our thoughts, prayers and lives.

With her aggressive chemo treatments only a week away, the next milestone for us was a CAT SCAN to set a baseline for the oncologist. The night before the scan we had a local priest, Fr. Jim Cosgrove (ironically initials of JC) came by our home to bless and anoint Debra. The very second he walked in our house he said he felt God's presence in our home. He went on to perform a beautiful healing service and left us all with a sense of contentment like no other.

The following day Debra had the CAT scan and remarkably the report read there was no mass anywhere throughout her organs. The weeds were gone for now! To add to this, the next day we received a second opinion from the original pathology. This second opinion differed from the original dramatically and confirmed the tumor was actually considered neuroendocrine and not pancreatic cancer, a much more treatable scenario. The original diagnosis was inaccurate and we now had a new type of hope in this incredible scenario. One of optimism and faith. We know our battle may not be over, but we also know God will have our back through it all and be our guiding force through whatever awaits us.

It goes without saying, through the numerous circumstances our family had experienced in just twelve short months our strength to persevere had been tested. Interestingly though, through it all, our faith increased daily and had been ignited, like no other, even at our lowest points. Debra and I both uniquely felt the power of prayer in both our journeys and truly felt God's presence every step of the way.

Through it all, we all had come to understand the powerful yet simplistic message of what little 18 month old Norah Petre saw in the waiving trees above through *Sway*. My hope and prayer for you is to feel the same presence of God as you travel through the pages ahead and experience Ryan Kerry and his own personal journey to better understand *Sway*.

Allow yourself to reflect on your own personal journeys as you follow Ryan. Through this reflection, my hope is for you to understand, regardless of the magnitude of your challenges and the weeds in your life, *Sway* can be your answer.

Acknowledgments

Debra, Brittani, Mike, Joey, and Anthony. The year 2018 and the beginning part of 2019 have been incredible times for all of us, ones we will look back on with favor as an inconceivable gift. We have been blessed beyond belief. Miracles do happen! My hope is to have *Sway* be one of those vehicles to share our blessed story and miracle. I love you all and am so proud of each and every one of you. You have all persevered through your faith! Debra, you are our miracle and our life. Love you!

We are also so blessed to have our family and friends in our lives. Each and every one of you came together for us in our time of need. We cannot thank you enough! We can only simply and humbly express our sincere love from the bottom of our hearts and tell you, without hesitation, we love and thank you all.

Special thanks and acknowledgements to DeAnn Bartram for your support and editing of *Sway*. Also, a very special thank you to John Ryan, Marc Petre, and little Norah Petre for your unique motivation and inspiration while writing *Sway*. *Sway* would not be what it is today without your participation. I can't thank you enough.

Enjoy *Sway*!

CHAPTER 1

Sway

A young father walked an orange-hue-lit path in the middle of a tree-lined forest, holding the tiny hand of his eighteen-month-old son. It was a quiet afternoon on the illuminated path when the young son pointed up at the tall trees and excitedly started to blurt out a bit of gibberish. The father kept trying to understand the various words that were forming from his young son but couldn't understand most of what was being said.

He looked down to his son and said, "What is it, bud? Are you saying *swim*?"

The young son shook his head no and let go of his father's hand to point upward and repeated the same gibberish.

The father said, "Are you saying *way*? Do you see a bird?"

The young son ignored his father's attempts at deciphering the gibberish until the father eventually said, "*Sway?*"

The young son immediately became content; he shook his head and said, "Yes," and rejoined his hand to his father's. They continued their peaceful walk on the orange-hue-lit path and watched the wind blow the upper branches above slowly back and forth. The father smiled at his young son and watched the tree branches move ever so softly as they strolled forward.

CHAPTER 2

The Terminal

The airline ticket read, "One way to North Carolina," as Ryan Kerry, a thirty-eight-year-old software engineer of Irish descent, sat in the terminal, waiting for his departing flight to arrive. Ryan, whose upper right cheek featured a large scar from a recent surgery, peered over to the way-finding signs posted on the wall to confirm his on time departure.

With fifty minutes remaining until boarding, Ryan gazed at his laptop with a blank stare as he began to daydream.

* * * * *

His thoughts brought him back to the origin of his surgery. It began with the day he first innocently went to the dermatologist to remove a tiny sunspot on his upper cheek to the fourth and final major surgery to repair his disfigured face from the hole the physicians carved while removing his small tumor.

He thought about how challenging the last few months had been, healing from his disfigurement to yet another ultimatum from his boss to move his family south or lose his job. He had been through a whirlwind of emotions the last few months, and it was finally time to prepare for his trip down south.

As he folded his last set of clothes and inserted them into his suitcase, he looked around his bedroom with scattered moving boxes in various places throughout the room and sighed. He walked from his bedroom to his large walk-in closet and passed by the shelving in the back.

A few pairs of shoes covered the various shelves, but they were also intermixed with a grouping of older framed pictures of his family through the years. From the condition of each photo, one could tell these were older Kodak moments and not from the digital age.

Ryan first passed by a full-length mirror in the back of the closet and quickly glanced at his face. It had become difficult to look at his own image since the surgery as he turned away quickly to avoid an extended stare at his scarred and asymmetrical appearance.

He stopped in front of the photos and gazed at the few memories in front of him. The graining photos were frayed and ripped, but each were intact due to the framing, which supported them. He gazed at one image in particular, which depicted a picture of a young father holding hands with a young son walking an orange-hue-lit trail in the middle of a tree-lined forest. The faces of the two could not be seen in the image, only the backs, as they walked the path. Ryan gazed at the image as if it was an endearing memory from his distant past.

He then looked over to the framed picture to the right. This one appeared much more frayed. It featured his father and a baby. In this image, the baby could not be more than eighteen months old as he sat on his father's lap. They were sitting on an old porch, staring upward at the tall swaying trees.

They both had such a peaceful stare and relaxed demeanor in the photo. They were clearly staring at something as the baby was nestled in comfort in his father's arms. As he gazed at the image, a small lump in his throat formed, and with a tight-lipped grin of bittersweet appreciation, he said, "Miss you, Dad. Please tell me I'm doing the right thing here," as he moved his attention to a third and final image. This was a single image of an old man, his grandfather. Ryan gazed at the image of his grandfather with the same melancholy look on his face and said to himself, *This is crazy, Pa. I can't believe I'm doing this again, especially after this monstrosity.*

He looked back at the mirror once again and glared at his scarred faced. He then looked at all three images and sarcastically said, "It really would be so much easier just to go back home again to a simpler time, with a simpler face. You guys were the best." He lifted his hand toward the image of his grandfather and touched it ever so lightly. "Say hi to Dad for me, Pa. Miss you, guys." He could see his scarred face once again within the glare of his grandfather's picture. "Man, this really does suck."

Ryan walked out of the walk-in closet and continued to place the clothes in his luggage when he heard his wife, Norah's, voice. Norah, an attractive thirty-two-year-old of Italian descent with long black hair, said, "Are you sure about this?"

Ryan looked up at his wife of ten years and said, "You know I don't have a choice. It's either this or I have to start all over somewhere else. I…I mean we are not doing that. We've come too far. Too many sacrifices over the years, not to mention too many corporate promises. But this one feels like the right one. Plus, I really do need a new start. We do this for a couple years, and then we can come back. I promise."

"What about my family?" Norah said.

"We've talked about this. We'll visit. They can visit. It will be fine," Ryan said.

"You really think my parents will visit us? They think going downtown requires a tollbooth, let alone traveling a thousand miles away. We won't see them. I guarantee it," Norah said.

Ryan put his clothes down and walked over to his wife in an effort to calm her down. He put his hand gently on her and said, "Then we'll visit them. We'll make this work, I promise you. Believe me, I've given up a ton over the years to get us to where we are. Leaving home for me was tough too, but I made it work. I didn't have a choice, and what I left behind was amazing. You know how much I think about that place, those people, that time. It was special, but I had to leave. It was the easiest and best decision, and so is this. Believe me, we'll persevere through this thing, I promise. And realistically, we don't have a choice."

"We always have a choice, Ryan. You know that," Norah said.

"I know, but in this case we don't. And believe me, I could use a change," Ryan said.

"I know you have been through so much lately, but leaving is not always the answer," she said.

Frustrated, Ryan looked away and said, "You know I can't deal with this now. Please support me here. This is the easiest and best decision. It gives us a quick way out. I gotta see it through. Who knows, this might be the move that changes it all for us."

* * * * *

Interrupted and nudged by another passenger walking down his aisle of seating in the gate area, Ryan was abruptly pulled out of his daydream and back into the airport. He looked around and back up to the way-finding sign. It read forty minutes until boarding.

He decided to gather his belongings and organize his travel bag. His laptop and various cords needed to power down and roll up. He systematically rolled up each cord he had plugged into the numerous outlets underneath his chairs and adjacent wall socket.

He had three cords, which had been charging his laptop, his cell phone, and his earphones. It took him about five minutes to fully close down each of his devices in preparation to repack his bag for travel.

When he finally closed down his laptop and placed it into his carry-on bag, he was ready to board. With a sigh of relief, he zipped up the last compartment of his bag and rested back into his chair and looked up at his fellow passengers who were also waiting.

He immediately noticed a large man, who was sitting next to three nuns across from him, react abruptly and said, "Aw, shit. You have got to be kidding me!" The man looked over to the nuns and quickly apologized for his language but at the same time pointed to the way-finding sign.

Confused, Ryan gazed at the man and then looked over to what he had assumed he was viewing. He looked at the way-finding sign and saw his flight had just been delayed three hours. "No way," Ryan said as he looked back to the other passengers. They were all now noticing the change in status with equal responses and reactions to the news.

He got up quickly and walked over to the gate desk and tried to get the attendant's attention. As he walked up to the desk, he had to dodge a man in a wheelchair nearby. As he walked around the disabled man, he said, "Excuse me." He then looked toward the attendant. "Sir, excuse me."

The attendant's back was to him. Eventually, the attendant turned around and looked at him. Oddly, the first thing Ryan noticed was the attendant was missing an eye. He had a large scar near his upper cheek, and he concealed it with poorly fitting glasses. The attendant appeared frustrated as he was doing his best to respond to the onslaught of passenger inquiries. "Can I help you?" the attendant said.

Not wanting to stare at the disfigurement on the man's face, Ryan did his best to look away and said, "Are we really delayed?"

The attendant saw Ryan shamelessly look away and in frustration and some insecurity covered his eye with his hand and said, "Yes, sir, it is delayed. As soon as we have more information we will announce it to everyone. Then and only then, will it be your turn."

Realizing his shameless look-away was not too well done, Ryan said in an apologetic manner, "Okay, thank, thank you." He turned away as numerous passengers followed suit.

"Aw, this really sucks," Ryan said as they all began to deal with the reality they had to wait longer to depart. They collectively moaned as a few more passengers scrambled to the podium to review their options. Ryan sat back into his seat, contemplating what to do for the next three hours.

Unsure if he should unpack his contents again within his carry-on, Ryan sat motionlessly for a few moments, trying to figure out his next move when he heard, "Well, I've always found alcohol is the best solution for moments like this." It was Gabe, the large barrel-chested man who sat across from him.

Chuckling, Ryan said, "You know, that sounds like a pretty damn good idea to me. Anyone else in?"

Most of the passengers ignored the two men as they looked over to one another and laughed.

"Well, maybe they'll join us later," Gabe said as he looked at the nuns amusingly and gathered his bag and stood up.

Ryan laughed and said, "Yeah, maybe."

As the two men got up, a few others slowly walked behind them and over to the bar restaurant near the gate. For the next couple of hours, Ryan and his newfound friend Gabe shared drinks by the bar as the others kept mostly to themselves. Every now and then, they would glance at the sign to make sure their flight remained on its new scheduled time. Gabe took a sip of his drink and turned to Ryan and said, "So what made you go to the doctor in the first place?"

Ryan sipped from his drink. "My wife, thank God. It was just a tiny sunspot that appeared to grow a bit. When I went to the first dermatologist, he didn't think too much of it. But the pathology came back melanoma, and the next few months turned into craziness. You see, with this type of skin cancer, they have to keep on cutting until they get to fresh tissue. At one point, I had a hole in my face this size," Ryan said as he made an oval with his fingers. "The last surgery was the craziest of all. The physician kept me awake for the whole procedure. It was a mini face-lift when it was all said and done. And, then I was given this," pointing to the large scar on his face.

Amazed at the story, Gabe sat back in his chair and said, "Wow. That's pretty intense. All from the sun, huh? Well at least they got it all out."

"Yeah, I suppose so. I mean I'm grateful and all, but this has been an interesting road, especially now with this new trip," Ryan said.

Gabe took another sip of his drink and said, "Yeah, so let me get this straight. After all of that, you're still going to leave it all behind and let your family just meet you down there?"

"I don't have a choice. My new boss made it clear I needed to be on-site in two weeks. Remote was not an option," Ryan said.

"Where you gonna live?" Gabe said.

"Oh, they took care of that too. Some special development they handpicked for us. Our HR rep said it was a life-changing place, and I'd thank them later for the opportunity. I haven't even seen the place, but I did get a call from my real estate agent telling me it was a lovely neighborhood. White picket fence and everything," Ryan said.

"Wow, that's a pretty ballsy move. I don't know if I could do that," Gabe said.

"Yeah, sometimes you just don't have a choice, I guess. Sometimes you just gotta go with the easiest path. Not to mention, I'd be out of job if I didn't," Ryan said.

"You know what, Ryan, you clearly have been through some shit lately, and you might think your

23

back is up against the wall with your job, but you always got a choice, man. Don't let anyone dictate your life to you. That's bullshit! Sometimes, it's better to be uncomfortable. You grow more. Hey, sometimes the roughest waters provide the best cruise," Gabe said.

"Easier said than done, Gabe," Ryan said as he stared at the bottles of liquor on the bar. "Hey, enough about me. It's too depressing. You want another drink?" Ryan said.

Gabe looked over at the way-finding sign and said, "Nah, I think we should finish up. Looks like we are actually boarding this time."

Ryan looked over to the line of people near the gate.

"Well, what do you know? That wasn't that bad after all. We're going to need that check now," Ryan said to the barkeep.

The two men gathered their belongings, and each paid their respective bills. Ryan looked over to Gabe and said, "Well, thanks for helping kill the time, Gabe. It was fun."

"Sure was. Hope everything goes well for you, my friend. It's good seeing you are still standing and smiling. Keep standing strong. I will be thinking about you," Gabe said.

"Thanks, man, truly appreciate it. Take care. Good meeting you," Ryan said as the two men grabbed their bags and walked toward the gate to board the plane.

CHAPTER 3

The Key

It was three weeks later, and Ryan was attending to his new yard again on the Saturday morning of Memorial Day weekend. It was a longer weekend, and he finally had time to work in his new yard.

Sweat poured from his brow as he pulled and ripped another weed from the fence. Problem was, every time he grabbed hold of the wild greenery, sharp thorn-like appendages scraped his ankles and wrists when he pulled from its root. "Son of a——," he said as he kept at his clearing. It weaved in and out of the chain-link and even knitted itself within the blades of grass under his feet. It was everywhere, and it seemed to have a mind of its own. As he pulled and dug, its thorns projected outward and appeared to retaliate. He felt as if he was at war with his own yard. This dance with the foliage lasted most of the day.

It didn't help matters as it was also eighty-five degrees but felt like it was well over one hundred.

The humidity was thick, and his body dripped of moistened dust from the dirt he kicked up from the frantic excavation.

This was the third day in a row Ryan cleared the area of this nasty weed. No matter how many times he came out to his new yard, the weed surfaced. It appeared to grow and spread daily even though he used every tool and weed killer he could find in his shed to rid his newly planted shrubbery and lawn from this pest-like foliage.

As he pulled and ripped the weed, Ryan marveled at the uniqueness of the plant. It felt more like soft stringy dough with hidden thorn-like spurs within. This was no ordinary vegetation, and Ryan was determined to find out why it had reappeared in his new house every day for the last week.

None of it made sense to him as he cleared the last of the unique greenery for the day. Typical weeds did not grow back this fast. Plus, the thorn attacks were starting to take a toll on his appendages. He surveyed the area once more following his extended weeding. No more weeds as far as he could see. He systematically picked up his tools and walked back to his shed as he tended to his wounds for the day.

The scrapes and bruises had mounted up, and he looked like he had run through a pricker bush unprotected. Tiny droplets of blood trickled from his ankles and wrists.

He surveyed the area once more with cautious optimism and finally let out a relieved sigh. He was convinced, at least for the day, it was gone and said,

"Come back again and I'm torching you next time."
Satisfied he had won the battle, he turned his back
and went into his new house.

* * * * *

Morning came and so did his frustration as Ryan
burst open the door to the backyard. He could see it
from his screened-in patio. The dough-like weed was
back. Less than twelve hours, and it was as if he had
not cleared the area at all. It even appeared to increase
in size.

"Unbelievable," Ryan said as he first went to
his refrigerator, grabbed his six-pack of beer, and
bolted toward the shed to get his tools once again. He
repeated the previous day's clearing as he dug even
deeper into the newly planted sod. Every so often, he
grabbed a beer from his iced cooler to fight off the
intense heat from the day. The thorns protruded into
his limbs as he pulled and ripped, but he kept at it
anyways with unbridled determination.

The task would take him most of the morning
and afternoon as he would periodically stop for breaks
to refresh his spirit with another brew. He would also
rinse away his ever-increasing wounds with the hose
nearby. As he rinsed his face and washed his wounds,
he drank from his beer as the neighborhood kids
played in proximity.

He wiped the excess water from his brow and
took a moment to take in his new neighborhood.
Ryan had only been in the house for three weeks now

and was still living by himself for the time being. The plan was his family would join him in a few weeks as they finished up school and finalized closing details on their old house up north.

Ever since his move, he had been consistently working on the house in some form or fashion, prepping for his family's arrival. He wanted it perfect for his wife, Norah, knowing she was sacrificing a ton to move down south for his new job. Until recently, he had concentrated exclusively on the inside. But with spring here, he was outside and decided to take a moment to survey his new surroundings.

As he looked around the neighborhood, a moment of relief came over him as he felt he had finally tackled this nasty weed problem for the last time. He sat in a nearby lawn chair and cracked open another beer.

As he drank from the can, he noticed a shadow near the chain-link fence next to his neighbor's yard. He took another swig and then noticed two of the neighborhood kids lying down near his fence. The kids looked about eleven or twelve years old and were hiding behind the shed.

They were chuckling in a mischievous manner, and as soon as they saw they were noticed, they hit one another and took off as if they were accomplices to a crime. "What the—" he said as he strolled over to the shed area. He watched them run down the street and looked to the ground where they were lying. Nothing out of the ordinary stood out until he saw a tiny shimmering reflection from the sun.

"What the hell?" He looked down and noticed an antique-looking brass skeleton key nestled within a newly formed cluster of weeds.

He looked back up to where the kids ran off, but they were long gone by now. "Huh," he sighed and decided to reach downward to retrieve the key within the new and fresh weed growth. As he grabbed for the key within the weeds, it was anchored to a stringed base. He pulled the key and the attached string weed upward and, as if he had triggered a booby trap from the attached twine, tiny thorn-like spikes shot upward from the ground and hit Ryan directly in his upper right cheek on his scar.

"Son of a—," he screamed outward as the thorn appendages penetrated and stuck in his upper cheek smack in the middle of his recent surgery. "You have got to be kidding me." He dropped the key back onto the ground and quickly tried to pull the thorns from his face.

He pulled on its base as a portion of the thorn broke off into his hand. However, the tip remained embedded within his cheek. "Aw, come on," he said in frustration as he frantically tried to pull the piece from his face. Unsuccessful, he anxiously turned toward the house and darted to his porch. Within seconds, Ryan felt woozy and had to stop for a moment to gather his senses.

As he stood in the middle of his backyard the world began to spin. "What is going on here?" he said as he tried to shake the cobwebs from his head. After a few seconds, the spinning ceased and his surroundings came in focus within his senses as he noticed something out of the ordinary. The weeds beneath and around him began to grow.

"What the," he said as the foliage weaved in and out of the strands of grass and made its way toward him. Nervous, Ryan started to move away from the odd growth to make his way toward his porch. He took a step forward, but the weed wrapped its way around his foot. "Hey, hey." He was in panic as the uncontrollable wild foliage spiderwebbed itself onto his lower leg.

"No, no. Somebody, help," he screamed as he pulled his leg and attempted to flee from the area. As he pulled away, the strands tightened and pulled back. Within seconds, Ryan fell to the ground on his knees. A second flurry of tiny thorn-like spikes darted upward toward his cheek and penetrated the area once again. Ryan screamed and immediately lost consciousness. As he fell to the ground, the uncontrollable weeds spread around him and engulfed his body completely.

CHAPTER 4

Awaken

Nestled in his bed with his sheets wrapped around his body in mummy-like form, Ryan awoke with a sudden rush of fear. His pillow was soaked from the sweat that poured from his neck as his confused nature of his surrounding confounded his morning wake.

He looked around his room and with a sigh of relief and a large deep breath said, "A dream. It was a dream." He sighed once again and aggressively pulled his legs from within the entanglement of his sheets. Once released, he swung his legs over and released another deep breath of relief.

"That was crazy. Should have never had that last beer," he said to himself as he placed his feet firmly on the ground. He stretched his arms upward and rose from the bed. He slowly made his way toward his bathroom to relieve himself.

He opened the door to the bathroom and walked toward the toilet, passing by his walled mirror. As he glanced over to his reflection, a rush of heat shot through his body as he double took a look at his face. "What the?" he said as he stared directly into the mirror. To his horror, Ryan's face had a perfectly symmetrical oval rash on his upper right cheek within his scar. Stunned, Ryan stared at the odd blemish upon his face in complete amazement. It looked as if someone took a shade of red lipstick and drew upon his cheek. He was utterly confused.

"What the hell?" he questioned his image in the mirror. Agitated, he maneuvered his face in multiple directions in an attempt to see if this was an illusion. With every move and gesture, the rash maintained as he stood in disbelief and concern.

He darted from the bathroom to the bedroom and from mirror to mirror, but the odd disfigurement upon his cheek did not cease. "I can't believe this!" he said as he stopped in his tracks. "It was finally healing. This can't be happening again," he said as he ran downstairs toward his back porch to look outside.

As he made it to the base of his steps, he turned the corner and could see the porch through his large southern kitchen. "Holy shit!" he said as he made his way toward the porch. The weed had grown exponentially. It had now overtaken the entire backyard and was nearly a foot high.

"What in the," he said as he surveyed the backyard from the protected area within his house. He ran from window to window across his porch and kitchen and could not believe his sight. "This is nuts!"

As his panic ensued, Ryan searched for his cell phone. "This is going to end today," he said as he found his phone and typed into his google search bar *local hardware stores*. A few stores populated within the search and Ryan focused in on the closest store, Paraclete's Hardware, which was just four miles away.

"I'm done with this!" he said as he grabbed his keys and rushed toward his garage and car. Quickly, he opened the garage door, turned on his car, and peeled out of his driveway toward Paraclete's Hardware.

* * * * *

As Ryan's car drove from the house, the back-porch door creaked open. At the base of the door, a tiny weed strand weaved into the house.

CHAPTER 5

The Road

Ryan accelerated the gas pedal as he drove through his new development with increased speed. It was early Monday morning on Memorial Day with no one on the street, which gave him increased flexibility to hit the gas harder. Within seconds, Ryan was out of the development and onto the long-stretched southern country road toward the hardware store.

As he drove, Ryan's mind raced out of control. *How am I going to get rid of this stuff? How can it grow like it does? What the hell is it?* His thoughts raced through his mind.

He drove past a few more developments on the country road. He kept the pedal to the metal and flew past the mile markers until he saw the sign up ahead for Exit 37 in two miles. This was his exit. He kept his speed up as his mind raced as well.

His questions of the odd weed continued as he felt odd sensations on his face. He looked up into his rearview mirror and noticed his rash had increased in redness. "What the." As he put his hand near his face, he also had a jarring revelation and quickly hit the brakes as if there was a deer in the road in front of him. His car came to an abrupt stop on the road and nearly tailspun out of control until it rested about a quarter mile from the exit. He threw the gear into park.

Ryan stared into the mirror at his ever-increasing rash and said to himself, "Wait a second. How the hell did I get into my bed last night?" Nearly hyperventilating, Ryan's breath shortened, and sweat dripped from his brow. He rested on the road. "What is going on?"

He sat motionlessly for a few moments until he was able to gain his composure. He slowly grabbed the gear and shifted it back into drive and hit the gas. He drove toward Exit 37 and Paraclete's Hardware, which was just a mile down the road in a small shopping center.

CHAPTER 6

Paraclete's Hardware

He drove up to Paraclete's Hardware and got out of the car. Paraclete's was a mom-and-pop-type hardware store in rural America—no frills or large department store feel. Paraclete's was your common neighborhood-like store where everyone seems to know everyone.

Still a bit out of sorts, Ryan threw open the front door and rushed into the store. Immediately, the proprietor, Alexander Paraclete, a large broad-shouldered Greek immigrant in his mid to late sixties, greeted Ryan and said, "Welcome to Paraclete's. Anything I can help you with?"

"Nah, I'm good," Ryan said in a rushed and somewhat rude-toned manner as he looked upward in the store at the various product category direction signs.

As he surveyed the categories, he finally found weed control on aisle 7. He rushed over to the aisle.

As he walked past each aisle, he couldn't help but notice the odd looks he had received from the various customers within the store. Each person he passed took an immediate double take in a slightly startled manner.

After the second and third look, Ryan became a bit self-conscious and bewildered as he searched the weed control aisle. As he paced up and down the aisle, looking at the various products, he kept noticing the odd looks he was still receiving from the people within the store. Finally, after a few moments of continual odd looks and uncomfortable stares, Mr. Paraclete came walking down the aisle as if Ryan had done something wrong.

In a self-defensive manner, Ryan looked up at the oncoming Mr. Paraclete and said, "Is there something wrong here?"

Mr. Paraclete stared at Ryan and said, "No, my friend. But you may need this." He reached out to Ryan and handed him a handkerchief.

Confused, Ryan said, "Excuse me?"

Mr. Paraclete pointed to Ryan's cheek and said, "You are bleeding my friend. Please." He handed him the handkerchief once again.

"I'm what?" Ryan said.

"Bleeding. Your cheek. You're dripping on my floor."

Ryan looked at his feet and noticed the blood droplets splashed on the floor and saw a track of them all the way from the door's entrance. "Oh my god!" he said in a panic as he swiftly grabbed the handkerchief from Mr. Paraclete. "Thank you. Do you have a restroom I could use?"

"Sure, it's right there in the back," Mr. Paraclete said.

"Thanks," Ryan said as he rushed toward the bathroom. Once inside, he took the handkerchief from his cheek. Instead of the rash, Ryan had what appeared to be a sizable chunk of skin excised from his right cheek once again. It looked as if someone took an ice cream scooper and gouged a piece from his face. It reminded him of his recent surgery all over again.

Stunned as to what he was looking at in the mirror, Ryan could not believe what he saw. "You have got to be kidding me!" he said as he stared at the large excision in his cheek. He dabbed away the excess blood, which had pooled on top of the wound. "This can't be happening. What the hell am I dealing with here?"

The door to the bathroom swung open as Mr. Paraclete strolled in with some gauze and tape. "I thought you can maybe use some of this, friend."

Startled, Ryan looked up and saw the gesture from the man and said, "What? Ah…yeah, yes. Thank you."

He reached his hand outward as Mr. Paraclete handed him the bandages and said, "Looks like you have been in some kind of fight, my friend, huh?"

"Fight? I guess you can say that. Problem is, it was with a weed," said Ryan.

"A weed?" Mr. Paraclete responded.

"I'm dead serious. That's why I'm here. I need to kill this stuff before it overruns my entire house. But now, I think it might be toxic. Look at this. That son of a bitch did this to my face. My scar was finally healing, and now it's back opened up again," he said as he revealed the wound once again to Mr. Paraclete.

"Well, if it's true, that is from a weed you're going to need a bit more than what's on aisle 7," Mr. Paraclete said.

"Do you think you can help?" Ryan said.

Mr. Paraclete handed him the tape for the bandages and said, "Clean yourself up a bit and meet me back in the store. We'll see what we can put together for you."

Ryan took the tape and humbly said, "Ah, thanks...ah?"

"Paraclete's the name," said Mr. Paraclete.

"Thank you, Mr. Paraclete. This is your store, then?" Ryan said.

Mr. Paraclete nodded with a grin and said, "I'll see you back in the store. Here's some ointment too. Should help with the bleeding." He tossed Ryan a small tube of ointment for his wound.

Ryan caught it and said, "Thanks again. I appreciate it."

CHAPTER 7

Paraclete's Advice

After ten minutes or so, Ryan finally came out of the bathroom with his wound bandaged up with a large bolus of gauze bunched on his cheek protecting his wound. Self-conscious, he strolled through the store as everyone and their brother stared at him as if he was on stage. Ryan felt the intense stares but kept on his way through the aisles in an attempt to find Mr. Paraclete. He walked hurriedly up and down the aisles and even passed aisle 7 where his blood had dripped on the floor. Remnants of the blood were still there but had been smeared over.

As Ryan strolled past the spot, he double took the bloodied area. The smeared spot resembled an abstract image of a skeleton key. Ryan stopped for a brief second but then kept on his way to find Mr. Paraclete.

Finally, after darting up and down numerous aisles and back and forth a few times over, he finally noticed Mr. Paraclete near the tool section assisting another customer. "Mr. Paraclete!" Ryan screamed down the aisle.

Mr. Paraclete glance over to Ryan but kept speaking to the other customer.

"Mr. Paraclete!" Ryan said again as he made his way over to the proprietor and his other customer. For the third time, "Mr. Paraclete, sir!"

Mr. Paraclete looked up and said, "Patience, my friend. It will be your turn soon."

"Sure, sure. Sorry. Finish what you have to do," Ryan said as he stepped to the side and let Mr. Paraclete finish speaking with the other customer.

Ryan waited patiently for one, two then three agonizing minutes as Mr. Paraclete and the customer kept discussing different sizes of tools for a shed the customer was building. Finally, after the third minute, Ryan interrupted again, "Excuse me are you almost—"

At that moment, the customer abruptly turned toward Ryan and harshly said, "We're finished here. It's your turn now. He's all yours."

Ryan looked up in an apologetic manner and was stunned to notice the customer had a deformed arm where he only had one tiny finger on his left side. Remorseful, Ryan said, "Oh, I'm sorry I—"

He attempted to speak to the customer but in frustration strolled right past him toward the exit.

Confused, Ryan watched him walk away as he heard from behind, "Has the hemorrhaging stopped, my friend?" Mr. Paraclete said.

Ryan turned back as Mr. Paraclete placed a shovel back on the wall near his tool section and said, "Has the bleeding stopped?"

Not sure how to respond, Ryan looked back toward the exit once more and then turned toward Mr. Paraclete and said, "Ah…yes, yes, it has. Thanks."

"Excellent. So how can I help you? You said you had a weed problem?" Mr. Paraclete said.

"Yes, yes, I do," Ryan said.

"What's it been doing?" Mr. Paraclete said.

"Well, about a week ago, I was cutting the grass, and this stringy thorn-like weed started to appear within the lawn. Every time I would cut it, it would seem to grow more. I'm really not sure, but I think it attacked me last night and gave me this," Ryan said as he pointed to his face.

"What do you mean you're really not sure?" Mr. Paraclete said.

"Well, the crazy thing is, and its kind a blurry because I blacked out, but I think I was out in my yard, and it sprayed some tiny thorny spikes toward my face. I don't know if I dreamt this, but I think it attacked me," Ryan said.

"Attacked you?" Mr. Paraclete said.

"I think it did, or maybe it didn't. I don't know because I woke up in my bed, and I really don't know how I got there. I don't know, but this thing is driving me crazy, and I need to get rid of it. Do you have anything that can help?" Ryan said.

"So let me get this straight. You think you were attacked by this weed, and you woke up in your bed, not knowing how you got there. Are you married, friend?" Mr. Paraclete said.

"Married? Yes, yes, I am. My family is up north right now. I just got a job here, and I moved in earlier. They'll be joining me soon," Ryan said.

"So you're by yourself now. Huh? How long have you been here?" Mr. Paraclete said.

"Not that long. Why should that matter? And what's with all the personal questions? I'm not here to be judged, sir. I just want to get rid of this weed. Can you help me or not?" Ryan said.

"Of course I can help you. Just trying to figure out what's going on. Were you drinking a little bit last night?" Mr. Paraclete said.

"I had a couple beers, but what's that have to do with anything?" Ryan said.

"Well, you said you weren't sure about some things. Do you think you might have had a few too many? I know how it could get when the family is not round," Mr. Paraclete said.

"Listen, I only had a couple beers. I was fine. Can you help me with this weed problem or not."

Mr. Paraclete reached over and placed another shovel back on the wall and said, "My friend, sometimes the weeds in your garden are there for a reason. Are you quite sure you want to pick them?"

"What are you talking about? Of course I want to pick them. I actually want to torch them. I don't think you know what I'm dealing with here," Ryan said.

"Oh, I'm quite sure I have an idea. You see, your challenge is quite common around here," Mr. Paraclete said.

"Common? This thing is common? Then what the hell is it? How can I get rid of it?" Ryan said.

Mr. Paraclete grabbed his final shovel and placed it on the wall and said, "This might be the type of foliage you allow in."

"What? Allow in? You're kidding, right?" Ryan said.

Mr. Paraclete turned away from Ryan and toward another customer waiting patiently for him and said, "I'll be with you in a moment."

"You're kidding, right? Are you going to be able to help me here or not?" Ryan said.

Mr. Paraclete turned back toward Ryan and said, "My friend, your help has always been in front of you. You just need to ask."

With a frustrated sigh, Ryan said, "Okay, I'm asking. Can you help me?"

Mr. Paraclete smiled and said politely, "Yes." He turned away and walked toward the other waiting customer.

Stunned, Ryan watched as he walked away and said to himself, "Unbelievable. These people are nuts around here."

Aggravated, Ryan looked around the store and said, "Screw it." He walked back to aisle 7, grabbed three extra-large containers of weed killer, and rushed to the checkout counter. He pulled out three twenty-dollar bills and threw them on the counter and said. "Keep the change…and your advice too."

Ryan stomped out of the store and threw the containers in his car and took off.

CHAPTER 8

The Trooper

Ryan was back on the road in no time at all. The streets and highways were still pretty much vacant as he pressed down upon the gas pedal.

He zoomed past mile marker after mile marker and periodically gazed in his rearview mirror to look at the bolus upon his face. The ridges at the base of the bolus had rims of blood, which had seeped under as his eyes peered downward. "This is unbelievable," he said as the speedometer hit eighty.

The car flew down the highway as Ryan said to himself, "I don't understand these people down here. That guy was crazy," as the car past the next mile marker.

Unfortunately, this mile marker had a police officer nestled behind a highway billboard. Ryan and his speeding car flew right past them. Out of the corner of his eye, Ryan saw the state trooper and said, "Oh, shit!" He immediately hit his brakes to slow down to fifty-five and looked back in his rearview mirror to see if the trooper had seen him. "No, no, no. Not today." He kept staring in the mirror and getting his car back to the legal speed limit.

With anticipation and a false sense of security, Ryan thought for a brief second he was in good shape until the lights came on. Within a matter of seconds, the trooper had peeled upon the road and with its lights flashing and pursuit in motion was directly behind him.

"Dammit!" Ryan said as he slowed down and pulled over to the side of the road. "This day just keeps on getting better." He pulled the car to a stop on the highway.

It took the police officer a few minutes to actually get out of his car as he took time to call into dispatch to check the license plate description. Finally, after sitting in the car, the state trooper emerged from the vehicle. Hidden behind his mirrored sunglasses and state trooper's brimmed hat, the officer strolled up cautiously to Ryan's car.

Anxious, Ryan peered his head out of his window and said to the oncoming officer, "Hello officer. Did I—"

Before he could finish his sentence, the state trooper said, "You in some kinda rush here, boy?"

"Rush? Ah…no. No, sir," said Ryan.

"Then why were ya speeding down my highway, son? I clocked you at ninety-two. This is not Daytona, boy."

"Ninety-two? Oh my god, I'm so sorry. I had no idea I was going that fast. Really?"

"Son, don't play the 'really' game with me. You know exactly how fast you were going. You gots yourself a speedometer right in front of your face. Ain't got no one on the highway this morning, but it don't excuse the fact you were speeding, boy. I gots to write you a ticket. Where you headed to so fast, anyhow?"

"It's a long story, but I'm heading back home to try to do some weeding in my new yard," Ryan said.

"Weeding? You were speeding on the highway to do some weeding in your yard? I think you definitely deserve a ticket. That's the stupidest thing I think I've ever heard," the trooper said.

"I guess when you put it like that, it does sound a bit crazy," Ryan said.

"What happen to your face there?" the trooper said.

Ryan laughed a tad and said, "Believe it or not, it was the weed."

"The weed did that?" the trooper said as he started to write out his ticket.

"It sure did," Ryan said.

"Well, then maybe you should go get that thing. I hate weeds. Did you ever try some weed killer?" the trooper said.

"Just picked some up at the hardware store," Ryan said as he pointed to his back seat.

The trooper looked in the backseat and saw the weed killer and said, "You go to Paraclete's?"

"Yeah, the hardware store. That's where I'm coming from," Ryan said.

"Well, if you're coming from Paraclete's, you'll get what you need. That stuff ya got there might work too." He followed up with a mumbled phrase and said, "But if I were you, I would stay focused on your keys, though."

Confused, Ryan said, "My what?"

The trooper ignored his question and said, "You need to slow down, friend." He then handed him the ticket.

Confused, Ryan grabbed the ticket as the trooper leaned over to his window and said, "Next time we see each other, let's not let it be over this, understand?"

Taken aback a bit as to the troopers demeanor, Ryan agreed and said, "Yeah, sure. Absolutely."

The trooper stood back up and walked away.

Ryan remained motionless for a few seconds as he watched the trooper get in his car and drive off. Finally, after a few more moments, Ryan, said, "I really do not get these people down here."

He threw his gear back into drive and pulled back onto the highway to head for his exit.

CHAPTER 9

Home

Ryan maintained the proper speed all the way home as he periodically glanced in his rearview mirror the entire way. As he pulled into his development, he noticed the two kids who were playing behind his yard on the side of the road near the corner of the street. They were standing near the sidewalk as if they were waiting for his arrival.

As he drove near them, Ryan slowed his car down and rolled his passenger-side window down to speak to the kids. Just as he pulled up to them, they took off once again and scampered away.

"Hey, where are you going?" Ryan screamed.

Within seconds the kids had rushed down the cul-de-sac street and into a neighboring backyard.

Ryan shook his head and said, "The kids are even nuts around here." He resumed his drive and finally pulled up to his house.

He glanced once more in the mirror to look at his wound as the bolus ridges had become even more soaked by some of the blood that had seeped. "This is ridiculous!" he said as he opened the door and got out of the car. He opened the back-seat door and grabbed hold of his packages from his trip to Paraclete's Hardware and walked toward his front door.

As he fumbled with his keys, Ryan put his packages on the porch and inserted the key into the keyhole for entry. He unlocked the door and swung it open. Immediately, he sensed something was not right.

Tentatively, he reached down and grabbed his packages and walked in. He closed the door behind him and proceeded to walk from his entry foyer into his kitchen. All the while, his uneasiness increased as the silence within the house made his discomfort amplify.

He slowly put the packages on the kitchen island and noticed a ray of light piercing from the back of the house inward. He also placed his cell phone and keys on the kitchen island near the packages. He crept forward in an effort to peak around the corner of the kitchen and into the family room near his screened-in porch.

At the edge of the kitchen's corner, he stopped for a brief second and took in a deep breath and exhaled. He peeked around the corner as his eyes grew to the size of silver dollars. "Holy shit!" he said as he stared toward his back porch.

The porch had been completely engulfed by the renegade weed infestation as the entire area was surrounded and covered with the green-webbed invader. It looked as if a forest had grown within his porch and backyard while he had been away.

Everywhere he looked, the weed had covered the structure and backyard. However, within its center, a bright light emanated from inside as the circular opening remained.

Ryan looked back at his pint-sized packages of weed prevention solution from the hardware store and immediately felt he may have underestimated the size of his problem and said sarcastically, "I think we're going to need a bigger boat."

The door to his porch was still open from earlier in the day as he quickly ran toward the entry and slammed it shut in an effort to provide a barricade from the intrusion. Instinctively, he locked the door and slowly backed away from the engulfed patio enclosure and said, "What is going on here?"

He looked around the porch and backyard and could not believe his eyes. His entire area and circumference of his property had been completely transformed. Everywhere he looked, it was a forest of weed-infested landscape. The crazy part of it all was the weed had grown inward and upward. It truly resembled another complete and different landscape, which had been overrun by a tropical forest of weeds.

The foliage was so vast, Ryan could not even see his original backyard or a neighboring infrastructure as it appeared he was looking into an entirely different landscape. He quickly scampered to each of his backyard windows within his house, and each view presented the same wilderness-like observation.

"This is nuts!" he said as he ran upstairs in an effort to see over the infestation; and as he ran into his master bedroom to gaze out the window, the foliage had made its way upward and out. All he could see was the tropical forest-like landscape, which had engulfed his property.

"I can't believe this. I gotta call someone. This is out of my league now." He suddenly heard a window shatter downstairs. "What the," he said as he reached down to his pockets for his phone and quickly realized he left it downstairs. "Shit!" He ran downstairs to retrieve his cell.

As soon as he made it to the base of the steps, to his horror, a thick weed strand had plunged its way into and around the house and had wrapped its tentacle-like arms around every access door in the house, essentially locking Ryan inside his own property.

"Oh no, you don't," Ryan said as he ran over to the front door in an effort to pry it open to flee. The tentacle-like weed was too strong for his effort to open as he panicked and looked around the rest of the house.

Every access point had now been jailed shut by the weed. Even the windows had been completely covered by the strong foliage as Ryan ran from access point to access point. Unsuccessful in his fleeing, Ryan ran back to the kitchen to retrieve his phone, which had been left on the counter.

As soon as he made it to the island, he stopped quickly to notice the phone was gone, as was the packages of weed prevention solutions from Paraclete's Hardware. He also noticed the door to the porch was swung back opened.

As he looked to the open door, standing near the bright light opening within the forest of weeds were the two little kids from his street. They had the package of weed prevention solutions and his cell phone in hand.

They both looked at one another, giggled, and proceeded to take off into the weeded forest opening. "You son of a bitch. Give me my stuff!" Ryan screamed as he ran toward the opening. As soon as he got close to the door's opening, he stopped in his tracks before going any farther. "Who are you? What is going on here?"

He stared into the bright white light opening of the tropical weed-constructed forest in front of him. He then looked back into his barricaded house. He turned back to the porch's opening and took in another very deep breath and said to himself, "This is friggin' crazy!" He slowly took a step forward into the porch opening.

CHAPTER 10

The Campfire

As soon as Ryan stepped onto the porch's entryway, the dirt beneath him circulated into a direction-leading manner and presented a pathway into the newly weed-constructed tropical utopia.

He continued to walk onto the dirt-covered path as the base of his foundation swirled and folded over and over forward as if it was showing him the direction into the path to follow. Uneasy but curiously determined to move on, Ryan slowly moved through the screened-in porch. He grabbed hold of the door's entrance and took in another deep breath as he stared into the long dirt pathway, which had now been overrun by trees, plants, and unique vegetation.

The trees lined the path and leaned toward the center, creating a tunnel-like entrance into the foliage. The sky could not be seen above due to the angle and coverage of the leaves. As he stepped onto the dirt-covered path, it continued to swirl in its directional-leading manner. Confused but intrigued, Ryan moved on and walked the tunneled path of trees.

"This is unbelievable," he said as he walked the path and tried to look within the lined trees to see if he could make out any of his backyard within this new landscape. The lined trees were too dense and the foliage too compacted for him to see within and beyond.

He continued on as the winding pathway kept moving the dirt beneath him. As he walked, he heard unique animal sounds within the brush. First were the sounds of the birds, then the playful sounds of squirrels and deer frolicking within the area emerged.

Ryan kept walking as the ground beneath him gently escorted him along, moving the dirt path ever so softly through its directional-leading swirl. Still uneasy but somewhat amused by the uniqueness of the winding path, he continued on. He kept walking until the swirling beneath him stopped. "Huh?" he said as he too stopped to look around.

Unsure of what to do, he remained motionless for a few seconds until a tiny red cardinal flew into his path. The cardinal fluttered around for a few seconds and appeared to stare at him in flight. It turned and continued down the path.

Ryan watched as the bird flew down the path and seemed to wait until he slowly followed along. He walked a few more yards down the trail toward a bend nearby. As he made it to the bend, he turned and saw the cardinal resting on a large boulder near a fork in the path. The fork led to two alternate tree-lined paths but also featured a tiny opening near its intersection.

"There ya are, little guy," he said as he walked toward the bird and the crossroad intersection. Interestingly, the bird did not appear to fear Ryan one bit. It remained on the boulder as he came closer. Only a few feet away, Ryan also noticed the small opening near the divided pathways.

He walked toward the opening and peered inside the trees as the bird curiously watched his every move. As he looked into the opening, Ryan saw a man sitting on a tree stump near a campfire with his back to him. Startled, Ryan remained motionless for a brief second. He then stepped forward off the path and into the opening and said hello.

The man did not acknowledge him but kept tending to the campfire while roasting what appeared to be marshmallows.

Ryan continued in and said, "Excuse me."

As he walked toward the man, the man slowly turned toward him and said, "Can I offer you a marshmallow, friend? They're mighty tasty."

As the man turned, Ryan was stunned to notice it was Mr. Paraclete from the hardware store roasting the marshmallow. Ryan said, "You? You're the guy from the…what are you doing here? Do-do you know what this is? What's going on here?"

Mr. Paraclete smiled and slowly reached to pull a freshly roasted marshmallow off the stick. He reached out toward Ryan with the treat and said, "Why don't you sit for a spell? Let's chat a bit."

Still uneasy, Ryan said, "Sit? I'm not sitting any-where until you tell me what's going on here."

Mr. Paraclete shrugged his shoulders and grabbed the marshmallow treat he had extended to Ryan and pulled it back and off the stick. He stuck it in his own mouth and ate the treat. He then placed another fresh one on the stick and stuck it above the fire and said, "You know what, friend, sometimes you just need to trust in your own heart and lean not on your own understandings. You just might find the winding path you're currently on may just straighten itself out."

"Who are you?" Ryan said as he moved a bit closer within the opening.

Mr. Paraclete looked up at him and said, "I'm a friend. Now why don't you sit down for a bit?"

Reluctant but accepting, Ryan walked over to the campfire and sat down on another tree stump near the fire.

Mr. Paraclete smiled and said, "Help yourself." He pointed to a few sticks on the ground near the stump next to a small basket with fresh marshmallows.

Ryan looked down and then back around his surroundings. "Maybe later. Can you tell me what's going on here?"

Mr. Paraclete rotated his marshmallow in the fire and said, "Well, at the moment, I'm trying to get the perfect toasting. You see, the key is knowing when to pull it from the flame."

Impatient, Ryan said, "Sir, I can—"

"Paraclete is the name. I thought I told you that?" said Mr. Paraclete.

"Paraclete, Mr. Paraclete, I can appreciate you have great insight into roasting marshmallows, but I need to know what is going on here. I'm about to lose it here," Ryan said.

Mr. Paraclete looked over to Ryan in a gentle but stern manner and said, "Patience has always been a challenge for you, hasn't it, Ryan?"

"Excuse me?" Ryan said.

"It's been difficult for you through the years to simply allow things to unfold, hasn't it?" Mr. Paraclete asked.

"How would you know anything about me? You don't know me from Adam," Ryan said.

Mr. Paraclete smiled and slowly reached to his completely toasted marshmallow and said, "Now it's perfect." He extended the stick toward Ryan. "I've known you for a long time, my friend. And believe me, you are a lot like Adam."

Confused, Ryan looked at Mr. Paraclete and said, "What?"

"Please try it. I took extra special care with this one," Mr. Paraclete said as he extended his stick more toward Ryan.

"Fine," Ryan said as he reached out and grabbed the toasted marshmallow from the stick and stuck it in his mouth. Within seconds he looked over to Mr. Paraclete with complete satisfaction and said, "Oh my god, this is awesome!"

Mr. Paraclete smiled and said, "There's plenty more. Help yourself." He pointed to the stick and basket once again.

With his guard let down a bit more, Ryan grabbed one of the sticks. He then picked up a marshmallow and said, "You know, I can't remember the last time I roasted a marshmallow. I used to love these things. These are fantastic. I don't remember them being this good."

"It was a while ago, wasn't it?" Mr. Paraclete said.

"It was. And if I may ask, you seem to know a little bit more about me than I do of you. Why is that? Who are you, sir?" Ryan said as he placed the marshmallow on his stick and stuck it near the fire.

Mr. Paraclete placed another marshmallow on his stick and placed it near the fire as well and said, "This is less about who I am and more about how I can help you with the path you're on and the one you have been seeking."

"Path? What path am I seeking? What are you talking about?" Ryan said.

Mr. Paraclete said, "Seems to me you have been searching for a while. Might be a little angry as well."

"How can you know that? And searching, searching for what? I'm simply trying to figure out what the heck is going on here. And yes, I'm getting a little angry!" Ryan said.

"Did you ever think the things happening around you are not happening to you? They may be happening for you." Mr. Paraclete said.

"What's that supposed to mean?" Ryan said.

"Could be all a gift," Mr. Paraclete said.

Ryan chuckled and said, "A gift? Yeah, right."

Mr. Paraclete placed another marshmallow on his stick and hovered it over the fire.

With no reaction to him, Ryan moved closer and said, "A gift? Is this a gift?" He pointed to his scar and wound upon his face. "How do I explain this? Can't imagine this is the long-lost Christmas gift I had been wishing for," angrily pointing to the wound on his cheek.

"You know, Ryan, sometimes a scar could mean your hurt is almost over. It could also mean you've endured the pain already, the healing has begun, and it may just be your turn to inspire," Mr. Paraclete said.

"Inspire? Yeah, right. How can this be inspiring? It's a friggin' freak show. You should see when I simply walk in a room. Heads turn to me like I'm a rock star. It's like they've never seen a scar on a face before. It's really ridiculous sometimes. People are something," Ryan said.

"Maybe they just are curious," Mr. Paraclete said.

"Curious? Yeah, I'll say they are. It's rude. I just ignore them at this stage. Truthfully, I would rather be alone than going into a room with people now," Ryan said.

"Forgive me, but you don't seem to be like that to me. I find it hard to believe you still don't like going into a room with people just because you have a scar," Mr. Paraclete said.

"You say this stuff like you know me, like you know my hurt," Ryan said.

"Your hurt is my hurt," Mr. Paraclete said.

"Who are you?" Ryan said.

Mr. Paraclete grabbed the marshmallow off the stick and stuck it in his mouth and said, "I told you. I'm a friend. A friend that brings help."

"Help? I never asked for help. Help from what?" Ryan said.

"Your search," Mr. Paraclete said.

"My search? Can you please tell me what I am searching for? I mean you seem to know everything about me. What the heck am I searching for?" Ryan said in a sarcastic manner.

"This is your third move in seven years, isn't it?" Mr. Paraclete said.

"Not sure how you know that, but yes, yes, it is," Ryan said.

"How's that been on you? How's it been on Norah?" Mr. Paraclete said.

Ryan looked at him in disbelief. "How do you know my wife's name?"

"Answer the question. How has it been?" Mr. Paraclete said.

"You're really starting to freak me out here. But okay, I'll answer it. First off, this recent little battle with this melanoma on my face didn't help matters. Damn thing wouldn't go away. It was like a weed on my face that kept coming back, but you seem to know that. And yeah, the moves have been tough. We've moved around a lot, but we needed to. I needed to be in front of the corporate brass to move up. You know the game," Ryan said.

"Well, sometimes it might be best to reevaluate if you are playing the right game at all. And maybe, just maybe, the obstacles you face are in front of you purposely to slow you down just enough to realize what's really important," Mr. Paraclete said.

"What's that supposed to mean? You saying this is for a reason?" Ryan points to his cheek. "This is some sort of gift to have me realize something? Well, I have to tell ya, that's one hell of a gift."

"Gifts don't always have to be wrapped up in shiny packages. Sometimes, they're presented in unique ways," Mr. Paraclete said.

"Well if that's the case, I'd like to return this one," Ryan said.

"You may think differently as you continue on. What about the moves?" Mr. Paraclete said.

"What about them?" Ryan said.

"Have they been worth it?" Mr. Paraclete said.

"Sure, we've increased our pay each time," Ryan said.

"Is it only pay that matters? Have you ever reevaluated what really matters?" Mr. Paraclete said.

"What do I need to reevaluate? I've always known what I had to do to move up. Norah knows too," Ryan said.

"Are you sure about that?" Mr. Paraclete said.

"If there is anything I'm sure about, it's that. It's the Kerry way. We keep moving, dodging them when we need to. And when you need to jump ship, you jump. If moving is part of the equation, then you move. It's how I've survived in corporate America."

"At what cost, though?" Mr. Paraclete said.

"No cost. We're doing fine. In fact, with this last move, I've gotten a fifteen percent raise. Not too shabby," Ryan said.

"So, no regrets, huh?" Mr. Paraclete said.

"Regrets?" Ryan said.

"Has it been worth it? All the moves," Mr. Paraclete said.

"Has it been worth it? Heck, I don't know. Yeah, I guess. I mean there have been sacrifices along the way. Some things I wish I could have back, but you can't live in the past. It's about moving forward," Ryan said.

"What if I told you, you can live in the past for a brief moment. Would you?" Mr. Paraclete said.

"What do you mean?" Ryan said.

"What if I told you I can give you one afternoon to spend a day with whomever you please? Maybe someone from your past?"

"When you say someone from my past, what do you mean by that?" Ryan said.

"It is how I have stated it. Whomever your heart desires. You can have an afternoon with them."

"Anyone? Living or dead, huh?" Ryan said.

"I'd simply phrase it as anyone your heart desires," Mr. Paraclete said.

"You can do that? You can give me an afternoon with whomever I please?" Ryan said in a disbelieving manner.

Mr. Paraclete simply nodded as he rotated his marshmallow in the fire.

"So, you're saying if I said I wanted to talk to George Washington or say John F. Kennedy, you can do that?" Ryan said.

"If that's who your heart desires," Mr. Paraclete said.

"Anyone?" Ryan said.

"If it is in your heart," Mr. Paraclete said.

"That's a tough question. Might have to think about that for a second," Ryan said.

"Do you really need to, or does your heart already know?" Mr. Paraclete said.

"How am I supposed to know what my heart knows?" Ryan said.

Mr. Paraclete smiled and said, "Just open it, and you'll know."

"I still don't understand," Ryan said.

"The path you seek is out there. However, as you can see, you are at a crossroad. There is an alternative pathway you can go down. One represents an easier way out, a shortcut back to where you were. Kind of a quick route back to your normal. The other path represents a road less traveled, but one that could be filled with the wisdom you have been missing. It's your choice, though. Simply travel down to the fork in the road and decide. However, once you choose one path over the other, you must stay on it to see it through. There's no turning back," Mr. Paraclete said.

"When you say an easier way out, how quick is the shortcut?" Ryan said.

"You can find out at the crossroad. It's your choice," Mr. Paraclete said.

"This is some kind of test, isn't it? An easier way out could be anything. I could fall off a cliff for all I know. And wisdom, what's that supposed to mean? Am I to go down that path and ultimately learn I should have chosen the other path? It's some kind of game you're playing here, huh?" Ryan said.

Mr. Paraclete put the stick down next to the marshmallow basket and calmly said, "It doesn't always have to be a game, Ryan. It's simply a choice. Why don't you let your heart lead you?"

"You keep saying as if it is an easy thing to do," Ryan said.

"Might be easier than you think," Mr. Paraclete said.

Ryan looked over at the two intersecting paths near the boulder and said, "Which way is which?"

"You'll know when you get there," Mr. Paraclete said.

Ryan chuckled as he stared at both of the pathways for a few moments. He finally looked back at Mr. Paraclete and said, "Any hints?"

Mr. Paraclete simply smiled as Ryan said, "I didn't think so."

Ryan put his stick down and walked over to the intersected pathways and stared into both trails.

CHAPTER 11

The Choice

He stood in front of the intersected pathways with a choice. As he gazed into each path, they were vastly different. The path on the right had an ominous look and appeared to have a storm brewing in the distance where the path on the left was calming and shining bright sunlight in the distance. Ryan stared intensively at each path for a few minutes.

He looked back into the opening as Mr. Paraclete had already turned away from him and resumed his roasting of his marshmallows. Ryan turned back to the pathways and said to himself, "I know this is a test. An easier way out could be anything, right? I mean it could be a quick path back home or it could mean millions of dollars or it could be something symbolic. And wisdom, what's that? I mean you could argue it would be wise to go down the road of possible riches as an out, right? Maybe that's the test here. If I don't choose an easier way out, then the road to wisdom will teach me the lesson I should have done. It's gotta be the easier way out, right? It's just logical."

Ryan contemplated his choice for a few more moments. He stepped forward toward the left path with the sunshine a few times and kept pulling his foot back. He looked back to Mr. Paraclete and said, "You said there's no turning back, right?"

Mr. Paraclete didn't answer as he kept his back to him. Ryan was essentially on his own at this point.

"I think it's an easier way out. The sunshine is definitely easier. This is finally my opportunity to get ahead of the game. This has got to be it," Ryan said as he picked up his foot once again and placed it onto the sunshine-lit path when suddenly the red cardinal reappeared and flew into his sight.

The cardinal perched on top of the boulder and seemed to stare at Ryan. Ryan pulled his foot back and said, "Are you going to show me the way, little guy?"

The bird didn't react as it remained perched on the boulder. Ryan watched the bird for a few seconds and said, "Nothing, huh? No hint from you either. What if I told you I'm going down the road to an easier way out, would you react then?" he said to the bird.

The bird had no reaction as it stared ahead. "Come on, give me something here," Ryan said as the bird did nothing. "Well if that's the case, then I'm going to do what he said. I'm following my heart. I think I'm going down this road of an easier way out." Ryan stepped back to gain his confidence to move forward.

The bird watched him as Ryan closed his eyes and said, "Okay, heart, lead me into this." He picked up his foot and went to place it onto the path of sunshine but suddenly switched it at the last minute and stepped onto the right-side trail with the ominous look.

As he opened his eyes and saw where his foot had led him, he immediately felt a sense of comfort rush through his body. Once both feet where firmly on the trail, the ominous surroundings suddenly vanished and the sunlight shone through the dense foliage above as the trail opened to reveal a tropical utopian setting with a stream and gentle waterfall in the distance.

Stunned at what had happened to the setting in front of him, Ryan turned back and looked at the alternate path he was close to choosing. The path had darkened, and a storm appeared to form in the distance with thunder and lightning emanating within. "Huh, now there's a switch," Ryan said as he looked into the darkened path and saw the red cardinal take off from the boulder and follow him into the his newfound trail. The cardinal once again flew into his view and fluttered in front of him. It hovered for a few seconds, staring into his eyes, and then suddenly turned and flew toward the tropical setting.

"This is crazy. Where am I?" Ryan said as a rush of complete comfort overtook his body. He took another step forward and followed the cardinal into the tropical paradise trail in front of him.

CHAPTER 12

Almost Wisdom

The sprinkling mist from a distant waterfall moistened the air around him as Ryan followed a burnt-orange-illuminated path in front of him. The gentle orange haze hovered and blanketed the base of the path, which shone from the sunlight in its distance.

The mist from the waterfall created a softer illumination from the haze as Ryan was in awe of the sight in front of him. He hadn't felt this good in years. Even his scarred face had a different feel to it as it began to heal from the environment. The crusted blood and recently carved-out wound slowly evaporated and transformed to his original healed scar from his final surgery.

Ryan truly felt a sense of relief as he walked the path. "Where am I?" he said as he marveled and walked the welcoming path. He felt so good within his core, he began to jog.

The path measured a couple hundred yards long and was equally lined with large tropical trees and foliage on each side. The gentle orange illumination provided a sense of calm for him as he soaked in the new environment. It was as if he was in a luxurious spa as he jogged down and periodically sprinted to test the rejuvenation he felt within his legs. He felt like a little kid again as he enjoyed the run along the orange-hue-lit path.

It would take him a few minutes to make his way down the entire path, and he enjoyed every second of it. Along the way, the tropical-lined forest around him provided the gentle sounds of water rushing and various animals frolicking. The farther he traveled down the path, the calmer and relieved he became.

As he neared the end of the path, Ryan slowed his sprint to a gentle jog, and then walk again. Interestingly, he was not out of breath as he could see an opening where the orange haze illumination morphed more into a gentle white light.

With only a few more yards to go, he stopped. He turned around to see how far he had walked and could still see the secondary path with the storm in the distance. He stared at it for a brief moment and then turned back toward the opening at the conclusion of his current path. With a large breath and feeling of exuberance he hadn't felt in years he said, "Let's do this."

He walked directly toward the white-lighted opening and crossed over into this new setting.

* * * * *

As soon as Ryan stepped foot into his new setting, the environment completely changed. Instead of being in the tropical-forest-lined paradise, he had now stepped foot on a concrete road in a small neighborhood in the suburbs.

"What the?" Ryan said as his startled nature stopped him in his tracks. "Where the?" He marveled at the change of scenery around him. He quickly turned to see if he could go back into the path, but the portal had closed, and he was now securely in a new setting in the middle of a street.

"This is unbelievable!" he said as he surveyed the area. As he looked around, a familiar feeling rushed through his being. He had been here before. "Wait a second, is this my old neighborhood?" Ryan had recognized the street from his childhood. He was standing in the middle of his childhood neighborhood. He looked up at the street sign, and it read "Sunset." It was his old street. "Sunset. You have got to be kidding me?"

The odd thing about the setting was it also appeared to be dated. He immediately noticed a puke-green-colored Dodge Dart parked in a driveway nearby. He had not seen a Dodge Dart since the seventies, especially one as ugly as the puke-green one he had noticed. His brother drove a similar-looking car, and the color was legendary. "A Dodge Dart. Unbelievable!" Ryan said.

He continued on as he strolled down the street. Everywhere he looked stunned him even more. As he walked the street, it was as if he was walking the same street where he had grown up as a child, and nothing had changed. The cars, the landscaping, and the color scheme of the houses were all the same. "Am I back home? Is this the real Sunset Drive I grew up on?"

He kept walking the street. As he strolled down the street, his pace quickened as his interest also heightened. "Is it still there?" he said as his walking sped.

He was now on pace toward where he had thought his old house was located. His swift walking turned into a light jog and then ultimately an all-out sprint toward the corner house at the end of Sunset Drive. It took him just a few seconds to sprint his way down the entire street until he made it to the end. As he passed his final old neighbor's house on their right, there it was. He stopped in his tracks and stared in disbelief.

His childhood home stood tall and had not changed one bit from his memory. The faded-yellow shutters and the black-trim garage door were intact and looked as if nothing had changed. Even the old porch near the tall Sequoia remained unchanged. "I can't believe this," he said.

As he surveyed the house from the street, he looked closer at the old porch and could see what looked like a man sitting on the swing in the distance. "No way!" he said in disbelief.

As he moved closer to gain a more clear view, the wind picked up and the Sequoia above the porch swayed. Ryan watched as the wind blew the upper branches slowly back and forth. Immediately a rush of déjà vu rushed through his body. There was something about the tree's movement that felt familiar, but he could not place it.

The closer he moved toward the porch, the more clearly the image of the man crystalized. It was his father. He couldn't believe what he was witnessing as his father, who had been deceased for over a decade, sat on the porch swing.

Ironically, the man on the porch—who was clearly his father—appeared to be in his late twenties to early thirties. His dark wavy hair and youthful complexion was odd to him, but there was no doubt in Ryan's mind this man was indeed his dad.

Only a few feet away from the porch, Ryan fought his increased nerves in an attempt to bubble up enough courage to blurt on his name and said, "Dad?"

The man on the porch turned toward Ryan and said, "Shhh."

Stunned, Ryan had noticed a baby in his dad's arms who had been sleeping in his lap.

"Oh my god, I'm sorry. I didn't see," Ryan said.

The man—Ryan's father—motioned to him to come on up to the porch and sit in the nearby chair near the swing. Acknowledging the gesture, Ryan slowly crept up toward the porch and nervously sat on the chair next to the swing.

Just as Ryan settled himself in, the weather surrounding them changed suddenly. Dark clouds appeared, and lightning strikes illuminated the sky. Startled by the sudden change, Ryan was distracted but at the same time trying to focus on his father and the baby in front of him.

Ryan's father looked up at the change in weather and swiftly glared back at Ryan. Ryan looked at his father's penetrating glare and had seen this expression of dissatisfaction before on his face. His father blurted out in an abrupt manner and said, "You took the easier way out?"

Stunned, Ryan said, "What? No, no, I didn't. I chose the other path."

With the same look of familiar dissatisfaction, Ryan's father said, "Did you?"

At that very moment the elements around him drastically changed, and the image of Ryan's father and the baby began to fade. Sensing he was about to lose his father for the second time, Ryan screamed, "No!"

Dark colors and flashback images rushed through Ryan's consciousness as he watched himself at the crossroads within the path, making his choice. He watched his unsure demeanor contemplate which path to take when clearly, at the moment of choice, he had convinced even himself he was going down the wiser path when in reality, he subconsciously chose the "easier way out."

When Ryan realized what he had done, he looked up to the fading image of his father in front of him and screamed, "Dad, no! Stay. I wanted this path. I don't want to—"

Within seconds his father and the baby vanished, and Ryan found himself back on his porch in his new house. The forested paradise was gone, and he was staring at a pristine backyard with no weeds in site.

Dumbfounded, Ryan screamed like a child as he stared into his newly immaculate landscaped backyard.

CHAPTER 13

Weed Ridden

As Ryan sat on his chair, staring into his backyard, he could not believe what had just happened. "No way. No friggin' way." He got up and rushed to the screen door and ran out to the middle of his backyard.

The backyard was now immaculate. There wasn't a weed in sight. In fact, the yard never looked so good. "No, no. Where are they? Where are they?"

He fell to the ground searching for any sight of a weed. There was nothing. The grass was so pristine, it looked as if it was manicured by a major league baseball team. Ryan scrambled around like a madman searching the yard for any sight of a weed. He could not find anything.

Finally, after running back and forth for well over ten minutes, he fell to the ground in exhaustion. His search came up empty, and he was back in the middle of his newly landscaped and pristine weed-ridden backyard.

He rolled over to his back and screamed outward, "I don't want the easier way out. Let me back in! Let me back in."

Nothing happened as Ryan lay on his back, staring up into the sky for the next hour.

CHAPTER 14

Lost Will

As the sunrays blanketed his uncovered and scarred face and arms, Ryan baked in the heat for over an hour as he depressingly rehashed his last few moments within the path at the crossroads. With his arms folded over his eyes in an attempt to block the rays from his recent surgery, he could now see himself clearly stepping onto the path to the "easier way out."

"What was I thinking? I'm such an idiot. I gotta get back. I gotta get back."

He unfolded his arms from covering his face and slowly rose upward as he sat with his legs extended within the middle of his backyard. He could not believe how pristine the yard looked, and the grass never appeared greener and weedless. "This is unbelievable. Not one friggin' weed in the yard. I can't believe this," he said as he surveyed the yard.

As he looked around, he also racked his brain on what to do. When an idea came upon him, he said, "That's it. It's the weeds. I need more weeds. I just have to plant the weeds."

Rejuvenated, Ryan jumped to his feet and started to run around the yard, looking for any sign of the unique weed. He scampered back and forth from every corner of his yard but could not find a weed in sight. "I can't believe this. For weeks, I'm trying to get rid of them, and now I can't find one if my life depended on it," he said as he ran to the front yard and then back to the backyard. There were no weeds in sight.

"Damn," he said as he rushed over toward his neighbor's yards to see if they may have any weed he could pull. It took him another fifteen minutes to fanatically run through his neighboring houses only to find pristine landscaping at each house he ran through.

Out of breath and nearly out of his mind, Ryan scoured as much of the neighborhood he could until exhaustion set in. Dejected, he walked back toward his house and slowly made his way back onto his porch.

He opened the swing door and strolled inside. As if he lost his will, Ryan sat on his chair near the kitchen table and stared out into his backyard and said, "What the hell's happening to me?"

He stood up and walked upstairs toward his bedroom. Exhausted and mentally spent, he dragged his feet directly to his bed and fell upon it. Within seconds he fell asleep.

CHAPTER 15

Stalking

The night came and went as Ryan slept like a baby, still in his clothes from the previous day. It was 10:00 a.m.; and like a rocket blasting off, he awoke with renewed passion and sat up on his bed and said, "The hardware store!"

He quickly jumped off the bed and scampered downstairs. He frantically looked for his keys and finally found them on a table near the kitchen. He grabbed the keys and rushed outside, all the while passing by his cell phone, which was back on top of his kitchen table.

As he slammed the door to the house shut, he rushed to his car in the driveway, and his phone rang. Never hearing the ringtone, Ryan quickly got in his car and pulled out of the driveway and headed back to Paraclete's Hardware.

The phone stopped ringing as the caller ID displayed, "Jim (New Boss)," upon the screen.

* * * * *

The car flew through the neighborhood and made it to the highway in no time at all. Ryan was determined to make it back to the store but also recalled his last time on the road with his run-in with the law. With his head on a swivel, he looked in his rearview mirror continually as he peered in every direction, looking for a state trooper hiding in the brush.

His GPS was set for Paraclete's Hardware as he raced through the highway. He kept glancing in every direction, keeping an eye out for the law while also peering into the GPS to route his course. Midway through the ride, his GPS rebooted. "Really?" Ryan screamed at the unit. He slowed as the global positioning system searched for the signal to continue his routing.

Ryan kept on driving as he periodically glanced at the GPS. He said to himself, "It was the first exit, right?" He saw the exit coming up in a half mile as he kept speaking to himself. "Yeah, it definitely was the first exit."

As he approached the exit, he veered to the right lane in route to the exit and ignored the searching GPS. "This is it." He drove off the exit and took a right onto the street. "There it is," he said as he saw the familiar-looking store in the distance.

He drove up to the driveway and slowly pulled in as he looked up at the stores signage and said, "What the?" The store looked identical, but the name of the hardware store was "Easy Way Hardware."

Ryan parked the car and tentatively opened the door. He slowly got out of the vehicle and confusingly peered up at the sign again. "I don't think I'm in Kansas anymore." He walked gingerly into the store and looked around. The layout appeared identical, but something was odd to him as he approached the first employee he saw and said, "Is your owner, Mr. Paraclete, here?"

The employee, a slender-looking teenage boy turned around and said, "Excuse me, whom did you need?"

"Your owner, Mr. Paraclete. Is he in?" Ryan said.

The employee said in a confused tone, "There's no Paraclete here. Our owner is some corporation guy out of New York. I don't even know his name, but he never comes here. Can I help you, though?"

"What?" Ryan said in disbelief. "I was just here, and I spoke directly with your owner. His name was Paraclete, and the name of the store was in his name. This doesn't make any sense."

"Well, I'm not sure whom you may have spoken to, sir, but our name has always been Easy Way Hardware. It goes with our slogan of, 'We help you take the *easy way out* of your hardware needs.' Is there anything I can help you with?" the employee said.

"Ah, no. No, thanks," Ryan said as he turned away in a confused manner from the employee and started to walk the aisles within the store.

About halfway down the aisle, Ryan turned around and said to the employee, "You know what, maybe you can help me." He walked back toward the employee.

"Sure. What do you need?" the employee said.

"It might sound a little crazy, but do you have anything that can help me grow weeds?" Ryan said.

Confused, the employee said, "Oh, sir, we are not that type of store."

"Not weed. I'm looking for something that will help me put the weeds that I had in my yard back," Ryan said.

"You want to grow weeds?" the employee said.

"Yes," Ryan said.

"Like the type most people want to get rid of?" the employee said.

"Exactly," Ryan said.

"Ah, I don't think we have anything like that, sir," the employee said.

Perplexed, Ryan said, "There has to be something. Where's your weed control aisle?"

"It's aisle 7," the employee said.

"Thanks!" Ryan said as he turned around and walked toward aisle 7.

As he made his way down the aisle, he read all the products he could, which were designed to eliminate weeds entirely. Bag by bag and solution by solution, they all read the same. As the employee stated, nothing within the aisle was designed to grow weeds.

"Damn," Ryan said as he kept on reading the material. "Come on, think, Ryan. How can you reverse engineer this thing? Can't be that difficult. I mean, weeds grow everywhere."

"You're telling me. They're everywhere," a voice from behind him stated.

Ryan turned around and saw a young woman standing in the aisle. "Excuse me, what did you say?" Ryan said.

The woman, an attractive thirty something brunette with a southern accent said, "Weeds. They are everywhere. I can't seem to get rid of them."

"You have weeds in your yard?" Ryan said in an enthusiastic tone.

"Yes, yes, I do. So many, I'm not sure what do with them," the woman said.

"Can you describe what they look like?" Ryan said enthusiastically.

"Describe them? Well, I really don't know. They're weeds. Just your common weeds, I guess," she said.

"They can't be common. Are they prickery?" Ryan said.

"Yeah, they have prickers. Can I ask why you are so interested in weeds?" she said.

"It's a long story, but I know this may sound weird, but would it be all right if I came to your house and took some of your weeds?" Ryan said.

Taken back and a bit freaked out, she said, "I'm really just here for some weed control. Nice meeting you." She tried to move away from him, but Ryan stepped in front.

"Listen, I'm not crazy. I just need to take a look at your weeds. I'll be in and out," Ryan said.

Now more terrified, the woman looked around for any help and said, "I'm sorry. I need to go. Sir, can you help me here," she screamed to the employee down the aisle.

"Please, I just need to—" Ryan said as the woman took off down the aisle in fear of his pursuit. "Dammit." Ryan watched her rush away from him as if he was a stalker.

She walked the remaining time in the store with the attendant as Ryan walked around dejected but also keeping an eye on her. As she finally went to the register after being escorted by the employee, Ryan left the store before her.

He rushed to his car and quickly pulled it out of sight before she came out.

As the woman finally left the store, she got in her car and left the parking lot. A few seconds passed by, and Ryan slowly pulled his car out from behind the store and began to follow behind her as she drove down the road.

She drove about five miles down on the stretch of highway, unaware she was being tailed by Ryan who had kept a fair distance between one another in an attempt not to be noticed. She drove to a fork in the road and veered right down a street that led to a neighborhood development. As she turned down the street, she peered in her rearview mirror and noticed Ryan's car in the distance.

Without missing a beat she reached for her cell phone and hit the gas. Her car sped down the street as Ryan quickened his pace to keep up. She traveled another couple of streets before turning quickly into a house near a cul-de-sac. She swiftly parked the car and rushed into the house.

A few seconds passed as Ryan slowly pulled his car near the house and put it in park. He got out of the car and started to walk over to the house. In the distance, he could see the front yard was riddled with weeds. He smiled and said, "Jackpot."

He quickened his pace and started to rush toward the front of the yard when he suddenly heard a siren and a loud speaker saying, "Stop right there."

Ryan turned and saw the same state trooper who had pulled him over earlier. He looked to the front window of the house and saw the woman was on the phone, looking out at the scene.

Ryan said, "No, you don't understand I—"

"I'm not going to say it again. Stop right there," the loud speaker from the state trooper's car blared.

"Shit!" Ryan said as he looked at the trooper and then to the weed-ridden grass. He was only ten yards away from the grass.

The trooper started to get out of his car when Ryan bolted for the grass. Within seconds Ryan dove for the grass and began to pull at the weeds. He pulled a few weeds out when suddenly he felt a jolt of pain shoot though his entire body as the trooper had shot a stun gun at Ryan.

Ryan's body convulsed as the trooper rushed over and apprehended him.

CHAPTER 16

Incarcerated

As he lay on the cot in the cell, Ryan stared upward. He had been thrown in jail for trespassing and public nuisance with intent to harass. This was so far from his actual intent, but he knew he may have crossed the line when he followed the woman home.

As he stared upward, his emotions were all over the place as he said to himself, "What the hell were you doing, Ryan? I think I've lost my mind. This thing is now out of control."

He stared at the ceiling in the small cell while waiting for the next moment an officer passed by to plead his case once again. It had happened three times already in the last couple of hours, and each time an officer on duty passed his cell, they repeated the same mantra of he would have to sleep it off and talk to the judge in the morning. Problem was, there was nothing to sleep off, and Ryan knew he was not intoxicated but had given the impression through his actions he must have been on something to act the way he did by following the woman and rummaging through her yard like a madman.

Each officer in their limited exposure to him would have none of it as Ryan would plead his innocence each time but to no avail; the police on duty simply would reassure him he was incarcerated, and he had better think about seeking legal counsel for his actions.

Ryan could not believe this had happened over the last few hours. He had to get out of this, but the problem was no one would listen. Hours would pass as he would pace his tiny cell and at times scream out to the officers on duty in attempts to plead his case.

No one would listen. It was now 2:00 a.m., and he was still up, staring at the darkness in his cell. Eventually, he knew he would get out of this and more than likely have to pay a stiff fine. He also started thinking about his new job and if this news would leak to someone in the company.

"How can I keep this quiet?" he repeated to himself as he kept beating himself up in his own mind and thoughts about his actions earlier in the day.

"This is so unbelievable. I need Norah. Oh, babe, I can use you now," he said as he dozed off a bit while trying hard to maintain his frustrated staring at the darkened ceiling in the cell.

As he dozed, his mind raced even more. It brought him back to the day Norah convinced him to see the dermatologist for the tiny sunspot on his cheek. It was an innocent visit to the doctor; but after the pathology came back and three surgeries later, Ryan and Norah were both in the doctor's office, waiting for them to peel off the bandage from his latest surgery.

As the physician's assistant peeled off the bandage, Ryan looked over to the mirror on the wall and saw a chunk of his skin from his upper cheek had been surgically removed from his face. He literally had a hole in his face the size of a golf ball. Stunned and in need of a reassuring glance, he looked over to Norah who had attempted to put on her best face but was equally stunned at the disfigurement.

Ryan was emotionally confused and devastated at the same time. In a matter of weeks, he went from tiny sunspot annoyance to a major disfigurement upon his face. Sensing his angst, Norah immediately shifted her demeanor, and for the next four weeks and through an intense surgery and face-lift repair that closed him up but left a major scar, she was his rock.

Norah provided the unwavering support and love Ryan needed at one of the most frustrating and confusing times in his life. Not only has he had to deal with the asymmetry of his face's disfigurement, he also had to deal with the overwhelming stares from anyone and everyone he would encounter. However, the one constant through his ordeal was the support and love he had received from his wife. When he was down, she lifted him up; and when he was unsure, she reassured him he could persevere.

As Ryan tossed and turned in his cell, the dream images and recap of Norah's support flooded his mind. His own demeanor as he lay on the cot also changed. Instead of the frustrated incarcerated-inmate feel he had beaten himself up with the last few hours, he was finally calming down from his remembrance of his wife and her loving support.

The last images that painted his dream-state mind were that of his packing before he had left for his job. He saw himself once again staring at his image in the mirror and Norah walking in, discussing the move and job down south. Just as he felt the reassurance of the support from Norah, he looked up at her image as she repeated her standard dialogue: "If this is what you really want, I'm sure we'll make it work." Her image was abruptly interrupted by the disappointing image of his young father holding the baby on the porch, staring at him, asking, "You took the easy way out?"

Startled, Ryan woke up. "No!" He immediately fell off the cot and onto the ground. He screamed facedown as the sweat from his forehead dripped off his scarred and still-blood-crusted face onto the floor beneath him.

As he lay on the ground with his head raised a few inches away, he was emotionally spent. His forehead kept dripping sweat mixed with the fragments of blood from his still-open scar onto the floor as he stared downward saying, "What is going on here? Someone, please, God, please help me understand what is going on."

He put his hands on the floor and leveraged himself upward until his knees provided the support. His head, still bent downward, kept dripping the sweat and blood onto the floor. Exhausted, he said, "Please, dear God, help me understand. I never wanted the easy way out. I was raised to be much stronger than that. Please, please let me back in."

On his knees with his head still forward, he stared at the floor watching the sweat-and-blood-mixed liquid splash downward. The darkened cell made it difficult to see the floor completely; but as the sweat and blood dripped from his face, he saw a familiar shape on the ground.

Intrigued, Ryan remained in the same position on his knees until the sweat dissipated from his restless state. Finally, after a few more moments, his head cooled enough to where no sweat emanated from his now-dried pores. He stared intensely at the darkened floor below.

It was dim within the cell, but he could faintly see the image on the floor from his unique blood-and-sweat mixture appeared to produce the same key-like appearance he had seen in the hardware store. It also resembled the key the young kids left in his yard a few days earlier. "What the?" he said as he moved closer to the ground to see if another angle gave him a more illuminated view. Still on his knees, he was able to move just enough to see the key image more clearly as more light shone from the hallway behind him.

The image was identical to the image in the hardware store and the key left by the kids in the yard. Ryan was dumbfounded as he stared at the floor and said, "Holy crap! Could I have had the key within me the whole time?" As if a spirited strength stirred within him, Ryan, with a dramatic gesture of renewed confidence, placed his hand on one of his knees and slowly stood tall within the cell. With his body fully upright and now standing firmly on both feet, he looked down the hallway to see if there were any police officers around. It was now 4:00 a.m., and the night shift officers were nowhere in sight.

With renewed enthusiasm, he rushed back toward the image on the floor and sat down on the cot. He leaned back and stuck his hand in his pockets and proceeded to pull out remnants of weeds he had managed to confiscate from the woman's yard before he was apprehended. He stared at the weed in his hand and looked to the puddled key-like image of his blood and sweat on the floor. He slowly dropped the weed fragments to the floor as they fell on top of the keyed blood-and-sweat-soaked image.

He watched in anticipation as the weed fragments rested on the floor. A few seconds were followed by a few minutes of waiting. Nothing had seemed to happen as Ryan's frustration surfaced once again. "I don't get it. Isn't this it? Isn't this the way back?"

At that moment, the weed on the floor moved. "Holy shit!" Ryan said as he watched in amazement as the weed fragments began to grow.

CHAPTER 17

The Harder Way In

Within seconds, the weed grew like a wildfire ignited by pure gasoline. It overtook the tiny cell in no time at all and quickly blew off the hinges to the cell door. Amazed once more, Ryan watched as the environment transformed almost immediately into the forestry entranceway he had witnessed previously within his porch off his house. He couldn't believe it had worked. "Oh my god. This is unbelievable!" he said as he shielded himself from the intense growth and wild transformation of the setting.

It took only a few minutes before Ryan realized he was no longer in the cell. The transformation created another portal and entranceway into a garden of mystery. He watched in curious but cautious delight as the forest entranceway made way for a narrow path out of the cell and into a new trail. He wiped off his excess sweat and fragmented blood smear from his face and slowly entered the pathway once again to follow along the new trail in front of him.

As he walked out of the cell and into the forest-lined path, he didn't look back. His determination this time around appeared more clear and focused as he increased his foot speed to follow the trail. The trail appeared longer than the last time he had walked through, and the forest on each side appeared denser. However, it did not deter his focus as he kept on looking into each side of the path, hoping an opening would occur.

"It's gotta be here. He's gotta be around again," He kept on trekking through the long and darkened path as he screamed out, "Hello! Is anyone out there? Mr. Paraclete, sir, are you here?" No response was heard as he kept walking.

He continued and tentatively said in a somewhat cautious tone, "D-Dad? Are...are you here?" Once again, no response. Not to be deterred, Ryan kept walking the trail until after another fifty yards, he saw what appeared to be another crossroad ahead.

There was no label or sign on either of the roads. As he made it to the edge of the crossroad, he stopped and screamed outward, "How do I know which one is which?"

No response once again.

"Come on," he said in frustration as he attempted to peer inside of each pathway.

He screamed, "Give me a hint here. I'm telling you now, I don't want the easy way out this time. Please show me the right path."

To his frustration, all he heard was the slight breeze within the forest around him. No response was heard. He crept closer to the path on the left and stuck his head in as far as he could to see within. The farther he peered in, the more he could see and feel. He immediately felt the warmth of the atmosphere around him and could slightly see a more tropical surrounding ahead.

He pulled back and walked over to the right side of the crossroad and did the same. As he stuck his head in the opposite occurred. Instead of warmth, he immediately felt a chill and could see and feel an intense storm cloud in the distance.

He pulled back once more and stepped away from both paths. He stared at both for a few seconds as he contemplated his next choice. He stood at the crossroad for a few minutes until he finally remembered a Bible verse his father had passed down to him, which resonated. He said to himself, "O ye of little faith. Why are you so afraid?"

Ryan stood tall and with confidence as he turned toward the right-side path where the storms were brewing ahead and proceeded to walk into the storm-ridden trail.

CHAPTER 18

Guardian

As soon as he stepped onto the path, he heard thunder, and the lighting didn't take too long to follow. With a bit of trepidation, Ryan continued forward without looking back at the sunshine-laden path to his left.

As he walked the path, the wind kicked up, and the rain started to fall. The farther he walked, the more the storm intensified. He was only fifty yards into the long path as the storm's wrath took over. The winds and the pelting rain slowed him down considerably as he fought to continue on. He screamed outward, "I'm not stopping or going back. This is the path I choose."

He kept at it for the next fifty yards as the storm reached monsoon-type levels. The winds were so intense, he could barely take the next steps. With increased determination, he kept at it as he fought harder and harder as the storm intensified with every second. "I don't care how hard it gets, I'm staying on this path!" he screamed.

Every step forward was countered with a step backward as the winds were so intense they almost lifted him off his feet. He kept at it with a new sense of purpose, which powered through his soul and gave him the will to continue on. "I'm not stopping!" he screamed as he fought the winds and pelting rain along the path.

The next few steps took their toll as the winds intensified even more. Ryan fought, but they were too much as he slipped and fell to the ground. With the rains pelting his face, he fought to continue on as he crawled forward. He crawled and struggled against the intense elements with all his might as he screamed, "Help! Please help me!"

He kept at it for the next few moments on his hands and knees crawling forward until exhaustion overtook and set in. The more he crawled, the more exhausted he became. Finally, he stopped in the center of the path on his knees. He reached upward to the sky and screamed, "Why?"

The rain pelted down upon his face as he had reached his pinnacle. He could go on no longer when suddenly, he felt a hand upon his hand.

Startled, he looked up, and to his astonishment, Gabe, the large barrel-chested man he met in the airport, was standing in front of him.

Gabe looked down at Ryan and said, "Come on, man. Remember, sometimes the roughest waters provide the best cruise."

Ryan could not believe what and who he was seeing. He said, "Gabe?"

"Let's go. You can do this. I'm here to help," Gabe said as he pulled on Ryan's hand to hoist him up.

With a new sense of resolve, Ryan slowly rose upward and stood tall. Once up, Ryan looked over at his old acquaintance and said, "How are—"

Gabe interrupted and said, "You want to chat, or do you want to get through the storm?"

Ryan nodded his head as the rain and winds intensified.

"Let's go," Gabe said as they started to walk through the pelting rains and winds along the path. Gabe's strength and girth helped to provide a much-needed shield and guide for Ryan as they plowed through the harsh elements. A few more minutes of the strenuous walk passed as they made their way along the long path. The elements would not cease in intensity; but through Gabe's assistance, they were able to near its end.

"We got this. We're almost there. Look!" Gabe screamed and pointed toward an opening.

Ryan tried to look up, but the showering rains made it difficult to see. It took a few more steps until he was able to see a break in the storm.

Within the darkness, Gabe guided him toward the light. They kept at it another fifty yards until the rains slowed and the winds eased. Finally, after what seemed like climbing a mountain, Ryan was able to see the break in the storm.

Gabe's assistance gave Ryan enough strength to make the rest of the way on his own. The winds had finally ceased, and the rains went from pelting to a drizzle as Ryan stopped for a second to look behind him. He could not believe they had made it through the storm along the path. It was still raging along the path they followed, but they had clearly made it to the perimeter of calmness. Out of breath, he looked over to Gabe and said, "How did you get here? Gabe, who are you?"

"You got strong faith, my friend. I'm just a guide sent to help you along your journey."

"My journey?" Ryan said.

"Yep. It ain't mine. You ready to keep on going?" Gabe said.

"Where to?" Ryan said.

"Let's keep on moving so this storm doesn't catch back up to us," Gabe said as he started to walk toward the cleared opening ahead.

"Where are we going?" Ryan said as he followed.

As Gabe kept his pace in front of Ryan, the drizzling rain ceased as well. Gabe said, "It's my understanding you been looking for some answers."

In an attempt to keep pace with Gabe, Ryan hustled up to him and said, "What do you mean I'm looking for answers? Answers to what?"

Gabe, stopped and looked down at him with a sarcastic look and said, "Come on, man. You know what you're looking for."

Confused, Ryan stood on the path for a moment and then continued on to try and catch back up with

Gabe and said, "No, I don't think I do. What are you talking about? What answers?"

Ignoring Ryan's persistent question, Gabe kept his pace toward the opening in the path and said sarcastically, "Oh just stop it."

Ryan kept at it as he rushed to keep pace with Gabe and said, "I'm telling you, I don't. I—" He suddenly stopped in midsentence, realizing Gabe had escorted him up and through a portal-like opening in the path.

They were back on a street at the end of a driveway, staring toward a house he clearly remembered. Stunned, Ryan said, "Oh my god!"

Gabe looked back at him and said with a grin, "Pretty cool, huh?"

Dumfounded, Ryan said, "This is my grandparents' house."

"Sure is. And if I'm smelling what I think I'm smelling, I think your grandmother just made some cutlets. You hungry?" Gabe said.

"What?" a stunned Ryan said.

"Come on," Gabe said as he proceeded to walk up the familiar driveway.

Perplexed, Ryan looked around the street and waited a second until he quickly followed Gabe as they walked up the driveway and into the open garage.

As he trotted through the garage, Ryan looked over to the wall. As if he had been transported back in time, everything was the same. From the old sink near the corner of the garage, to the tools on their hooks, to finally the ancient rotary phone hanging on the wall, it was all the same. "Unbelievable," he said as he watched Gabe walk into the house his grandparents had lived in. He waited a few seconds to take in the sights and then finally walked in.

CHAPTER 19

The Cutlets

It didn't take long for the familiar smell of his grand-mother's breaded cutlets to penetrate his senses. "No way," Ryan said as he walk in the house. The tiny house didn't have much to it as the kitchen was the first room from the garage. Gabe stood near the old stove with a piece of the thinly cut breaded cutlets in his hand. He had already taken a bite. "These are phenomenal."

The kitchen was empty other than the two of them as Gabe stood and enjoyed the food that was made. In awe as to where he was, Ryan looked around the kitchen and marveled at how everything was the same to him. He slowly walked around the tiny room and even looked within the refrigerator for old times' sake. As he opened the door, he chuckled as he saw grapefruits cut in half, a variety of cheeses, and Blatz beer on the shelves. He closed the door and looked up at Gabe and said, "This is crazy."

With his mouth full, Gabe said, "You gonna have any of these? If not, I might not be able to stop. They're too good. And the paper-thin way they're made, they're like—"

"Potatoes chips," Ryan finished his sentence.

"Yeah, just awesome," Gabe said.

"That was my grandmother's specialty. She pounded the chicken all day just to get them to be so thin," Ryan said as he walked over toward the stove and grabbed a cutlet. He proceeded to place the cutlet in his mouth; and as he took a bite, his taste buds went on a ride back in time. "Oh my god." With every bite he took, he had been transported back to the memories of his past. "I can't believe this."

For the next few moments, the two of them devoured the plate of cutlets on the stove. As they ate, Ryan took a plate with him and sat at the familiar kitchen table from his early childhood and ate the remaining cutlets with his hand. He said, "This is nuts. I remember sitting at this table. I think it was always this chair too. My grandfather would always sit there," pointing to the chair near the wall at the head. "My grandmother never sat. Always stood by the stove. You know, I honestly can't remember her ever sitting with us."

Gabe smiled as Ryan reminisced. He looked over to the front room, which was adjacent to the kitchen and said, "I think she's sitting now."

Ryan looked at him perplexed and said, "What did you say?"

"Sitting. She's sitting now. Take a look," Gabe said as he motioned his head toward the front room.

Not quite sure what to do or how to take what Gabe just said, Ryan slowly rose from his chair and walked tentatively to the door's opening near the kitchen and front room entrance. He peered his head around the corner and, as if he was seven years old again, he was staring at his grandparents sitting in their respective armchairs, watching television.

They were watching Big Time Wrestling, a favorite of his grandfather's. This was a moment he had experienced numerous times in his past. They always sat in the same chairs and would always watch the same programs. Funny thing was, his grandfather was the one watching the show as his grandmother would either stare forward daydreaming or knit a blanket. Today, she was knitting a familiar blanket.

Ryan stared at the two of them for a few seconds without uttering a word until finally, his grandmother said to him without turning her head, "Did you put your dish in the sink?"

Startled, Ryan said, "Excuse me?"

"The sink. Did you put your dish in the sink?" his grandmother said.

"Ah, no, but let me get right on it," Ryan rushed over to the table and grabbed his dish and quickly put it in the sink. As he turned around, he noticed Gabe was gone. He looked around the kitchen, and there were no signs of his big friend. Confused but going with the moment, he rushed back to the entrance to the front room and peered back in.

His grandparents were still in the room. He slowed down and timidly stepped into the tiny rectangle-shaped front room. The large 1970 Magnavox television was against the far wall as the front room featured a long couch covered completely in heavy-duty plastic to protect from stains.

As Ryan walked in, his grandparents did not overreact to his being in the room. They kept to their current activities of knitting and watching Big Time Wrestling. Unsure of what to do, Ryan walked past them in awe and cautiously sat on the heavy plastic-covered couch against the wall. He looked around the room and it felt as if he was in a dream looking at the two of them. Finally, after a few seconds of uncertainty, Ryan's grandfather looked away from the television and turned to Ryan with a smile on his face and said, "How's my boy?"

As if the weight of the world lifted from his shoulders, Ryan let out a sigh of relief and said, "I'm doing great, Pa. How are you?" He got up and rushed over to his grandfather and gave him a big hug. He then turned and did the same to his grandmother and said, "Nanny!"

The three embraced as if they had not seen each other in a while, and Ryan could not help but shed a tear of joy as he felt the same bearded stubble face of his grandfather and noticed the same standard apron his grandmother wore pretty much forever.

Ryan stood up and said with a tear dripping from his face, "I can't believe what I am seeing. You guys haven't changed. Is this real? Am I dreaming?"

"Dreaming? Why would you be dreaming? Have you been having trouble sleeping lately?" his grandmother said.

"No, no, not at all. I'm just saying this is all so surreal. Am I in heaven?"

"Kinda looks like our living room to me. Did you get enough to eat? Can I make you something else? I'm going to make you some pasta. That'll fill you up," she said.

"No, I'm really fine," Ryan said.

"You're not fine. That's why you're here. I'm going to make you some pasta," she said as she got up from her armchair.

"No, Nanny, really!" Ryan said as she completely ignored him and shuffled to the kitchen.

"You know better than to try and stop her, my boy. Why don't you sit down for a bit?" Pa said.

"Yeah, yeah, okay," Ryan said in a more confused manner as he hesitantly made his way over to the plastic-covered couch and sat down.

"Can you believe Andre the Giant is losing to Johnny Powers again? He's got to be sick or something," Pa said as he pointed to the television.

Ryan looked over to the television and said, "You do know this is fixed, Pa. They make it all up."

"That's hogwash. The only thing that's fixed is politics. These are finely tuned athletes showcasing their skills, and don't you forget that," Pa said.

Antsy, Ryan got up from the couch and walked over to the television and turned down the sound.

He turned to his grandfather and innocently said, "Pa, where am I? What's going on here?"

His grandfather smiled and said, "You've been hurting lately, haven't you been, my boy?"

"It's been a couple tough months, but I'm moving through it," Ryan said.

"Are you?" Pa said.

"Yeah, I think I am. Got a new job, a new house that has a little bit of a weed problem, but it's new, nonetheless. And I'm healing…kind of," Ryan said.

"What about Norah?" Pa said.

"Norah?" Ryan said.

"Yes, Norah. How has she been with all of this?" Pa said.

"Great. I mean, really great. I don't think I could have made it through without her," Ryan said.

"Then why did you leave her?" Pa said.

"I didn't leave her. It just didn't time out right with the sale of the house and the kids' school," Ryan said.

"Were all the moves necessary, or just easier for you?" Pa said.

"Yeah, they were necessary. I had to each time, or I was out of a job. And believe me, none of it was easy. From the skin cancer to the new jobs, it's been a fight every day, every year. And one I feel, quite honestly, like I'm fighting on my own all the time," Ryan said.

"Ever think that might be the issue?" Pa said.

"What do you mean?" Ryan said.

"You've forgotten," Pa said.

"Forgotten? Forgotten what?" Ryan said.

"You saw it years ago. In fact, you taught us all how to see it and embrace it," Pa said.

"What are you talking about?" Ryan said.

"You really don't remember?" Pa said.

"I honestly do not have a clue to what you are talking about," Ryan said.

Just then, Nanny popped her head back into the room and said, "Pasta is ready."

"Pasta? Nanny, no, I'm not—"

She interrupted him and said, "Why don't you see if you're father wants some too. I'll keep it warm on the stove."

Stunned as to what he just heard, Ryan looked up at his grandmother in the doorway and said, "What did you just say?"

"Go and see if your father wants some too. He's outside by the porch," she said.

"My father is outside?" Ryan said with enthusiasm.

"By the porch. See if wants something," she said.

Ryan looked over to his grandfather and said, "What have I forgotten?"

His grandfather looked up at him and said, "See if your dad wants to take a walk on the path again. Might help you to remember. He's on the porch."

Confused but excited, Ryan turned and made a beeline to exit near the porch.

CHAPTER 20

Dad

The porch was immediately off to the right of the front door. As soon as he opened the door, Ryan's expectations rose. The door creaked as he swung it open, and Ryan stepped onto the porch. As he looked around, it was empty. However, he saw the porch swing was moving back and forth as if it was recently used. Curious, he walked over to the swing and stopped it with his hand. He looked around his surroundings and immediately felt the déjà vu of the moment.

This setting was very familiar to him. Ryan sat down on the swing and stared forward. In the distance, he could see the path his grandfather had just mentioned. As he stared more at the trail, the image of the old picture in his closet came to mind. Ryan could picture the grainy old image of the father and young son walking the path with their backs to the camera. As he stared at the path, he said to himself, "The old image. It's the same path."

From behind him and off of the porch a voice said, "Sure is."

Startled, Ryan turned and saw his father standing off the porch. He was older than what he had recently seen, and he was by himself this time without the baby. Not sure on how to react, Ryan stood up and said, "Dad? Is it really you?"

In a nonthreatening manner, his father walked around the porch near the steps, opened his arms, and said, "Hi, bud. Yes, it's really me. Please don't be startled. You've been through enough already."

His father walked up the porch as Ryan said, "I can't believe it." He rushed over to him as the two embraced as if they hadn't seen each other in years.

As Ryan looked into his eyes, he said, "This is crazy. I think I'm losing my mind."

As they let go of one another, his father said, "You're not losing your mind. You've just been blessed with a little sneak peek of things. You've got a great message. Just might need a little help in delivering it. Not to mention, you clearly did not take the easy way out this time."

"No. No. I didn't," Ryan said as his father walked over to the swing and sat down.

Ryan turned to his father and said, "What do you mean by sneak peek, and what message?"

"Why don't you sit down, and we can talk," his father said.

"All right," Ryan said as he walked over and sat next to him on the swing. He looked over to his father. "Dad, where am I? How is all this possible?"

His father looked out near the tree-lined path and said, "You're back home, bud."

"I understand that, but, Dad, you passed away almost fifteen years ago. Am I dead too?" Ryan asked.

"Far from it, son. No. It's just your time to truly realize your purpose," his father said.

"My purpose? What do you mean?" Ryan said.

"We all have our purpose. Some know it from the beginning, some take all their life to realize it, some unfortunately never find it, and some just need to be reminded of what they truly knew from the start, how they inspired others and didn't even know," his father said.

"So which one am I?" Ryan said.

"As you think about the last few years, what has been your constant?" his father said.

Ryan looked at him and wasn't quite sure where he was going and said, "I don't know. We have moved a lot. I guess moving."

"A little bit deeper than that," his father said.

"Well, if you want the truth, the one constant has been worry. I haven't been comfortable in years. always worrying about the next job, worrying about how I can provide for Norah and the kids and how we are going to pay for school for the kids. It's been a grind. If you want a constant, I guess that's pretty constant. It never goes away. And then, just when I feel I might be getting somewhere, I get hit with this

113

thing," he points to his face. "So not only do I have to worry about another job, I look like I have been hit by a truck 24-7. So it's been a real fun party lately."

"You haven't complained a lot," his father said.

"Complain? Who would I complain to? I could never let Norah see this pain. And the kids are too young. No way am I going to let on to them. No, I push through it. And if I have to make a move, I do. Perseverance, right? If I remember, I may have learned that from someone I know," Ryan said.

"You clearly have persevered, but have you thought about the road you've taken to persevere?" his father said.

"What do you mean?" Ryan said.

"When you had a choice at the crossroads, what did you do?" his father said.

"That wasn't my fault. I meant to go the other path," Ryan said.

"Which road did you choose?" his father said.

"I know. It was the easier way out," Ryan said.

"Might be a constant," his father said.

"Aw, come on! That's not fair. I don't take the easy way out all the time," Ryan said.

"I'm not saying you do, but sometimes, the tougher roads lead you to the better outcome. The weeds in our life might just be there for a reason. You pick at them too much, they may just overtake everything," his father said.

"So what am I supposed to do, ignore the weeds in my life?" Ryan said.

"Don't ignore them. Embrace them. They are there for you," his father said.

"So this weed on my face was for me, huh?" Ryan said as he pointed to his scar.

"Inspiration can come in all different forms. When you have an opportunity to inspire, my son, you have always been the one to take it," his father said.

"Inspire? How can this inspire?" Ryan said.

"You have forgotten, haven't you?" his father said.

"What are you guys talking about? Pa just said the same thing. Forgotten what?" Ryan said.

"It was you who inspired us all, and it was on that path. Don't you remember?" his father said.

"That path?" Ryan said as he pointed to the tree-lined path.

"That very one," his father said.

Ryan stood up and walked to the edge of the porch and stared at the path and said, "I mean, I remember the path, but I'm not getting what you two want me to remember."

"Give it a little time. Do you remember what you said?" his father said.

"What I said? To whom?" Ryan asked.

"You and I went for a walk. You were about eighteen months old," his father said.

"Eighteen months old? Are you kidding me? How would I remember what I said when I was eighteen months old?" Ryan said.

"You felt it then, you could feel it now. Why don't you take a walk and see," his father said.

"A walk? You want me to take a walk on the path?" Ryan said.

"It'll be fine," his father said.

"Are you coming?" Ryan said.

"We'll join you eventually. For now, just let the path bring you to where you need to go," his father said.

"Wait a second, will I see you again?" Ryan said.

"Of course you will. But for now, you need to remember. Go ahead. Go find your purpose," his father said.

Realizing he may be saying goodbye to his father again, Ryan rushed over to him and said, "Dad, I don't want to say goodbye again. We just came together."

"It's not goodbye. I promise you that. Now go. Your time is now," his father said.

Ryan looked over to the path and then back to his father. He hugged him with all his might and said, "I miss you, Dad."

"I miss you too, son. But know that we are always one. I'm always there. But today, you need to keep moving," his father said.

With a tear in his eye, Ryan looked back over to the path and said, "All right. I hope I find what you want me to. I hope I can remember."

"Just keep your heart open, and you'll see," his father said.

Ryan turned back to him once more and gave him one last hug. As his father looked him in the eyes and said, "I'm proud of you, son. I've always been. Now go and find your purpose."

"Love you, Dad," Ryan said.

"Love you, Ryan," his father said as Ryan turned toward the path and walked toward the orange hue lit trail.

CHAPTER 21

The Path

Ryan stepped on the path and started to walk. He turned back toward his father now joined by his grandparents on the porch. With a gentle wave, they provided enough motivation for him to continue on as they smiled and sat down, watching him stroll down the trail. Ryan waved back to them and then turned away. The path's orange-hue-lit illumination set the tone for his walk as he continued forward, unsure of what to expect.

He walked for a couple minutes with nothing happening on either side of the path or in front of him. Confused, he said, "I don't understand. What is supposed to happen here? What am I supposed to remember?"

He continued his walk, but utter silence and stillness remained. Finally, after a couple more minutes of walking in silence he stopped, looked upward and screamed, "I don't understand! Help me. Help me to remember!" Within a few seconds a gentle breeze brushed over him and through the path. As the breeze flowed, Ryan noticed the branches and leaves of the trees swaying.

As the motion of the branches gently moved from side to side, he suddenly had a rush of emotions, which filled his body. The movement of the trees triggered a rush of memories from his early childhood. As if he were watching old movies, he remembered tiny aspects of his childhood and varied times with his family. He saw the good times and the bad.

The good times flooded his memory banks as he smiled and watched as he played with his siblings and friends as well as special moments with his parents. He also remembered the bad times. He saw some of the tragic moments of losing cousins in car accidents, to his parents' losing their jobs, to diseases that ultimately shook them all. It was this final memory that flooded his mind the most. It was of the time he had learned of his grandfather's sickness.

It was then he saw the path through this same memory. The memory became clearer. It was the day his grandfather would come home with the news he had cancer. The family was devastated, and many found recluse in their own ways of solitude. But it was the path on where Ryan would hear the news from his father directly. The oddness of the moment was that Ryan was only eighteen months old when the walk occurred. His father was so devastated from the news, the walk became a catharsis for him as he walked with his young son on the path.

Ryan would remember the walk. His father simply held his hand as they walked along the trail. Not much was said as they walked along the tree-lined path as his father's demeanor was clearly down due to the news he had just received. The young Ryan watched his somber father intently as they walked a bit more when his father finally looked up to the sky and said, "Oh I don't understand this. Why is this happening to us? Why does this happen to anyone? Why all this pain? Help me understand."

As they continued to walk, the young Ryan pointed up at the tall trees and excitedly started to blurt out a bit of gibberish. His father kept trying to understand the various words that were forming from his young son but couldn't understand most of what was being said. He looked down to his son and said, "What is it, bud? Are you saying 'swim'?"

Ryan shook his head no and let go of his father's hand to point upward and repeated the same gibberish.

His father said, "Are you saying 'way'? Do you see a bird?"

Ryan ignored his father's attempts at deciphering the gibberish until his father eventually said, "*Sway?*"

Ryan immediately became content and said yes and rejoined his hand to his father's. At that moment, a rush of contentment filled his father as he simply looked up, smiled, and said to himself, "*Sway*," As they continued their walk along the path.

Ryan awoke from his memory-driven daydream as he found himself back on the path, staring up at the trees. He watched as the trees moved in the wind, and he smiled to himself and said, "*Sway!*"

As he looked back on the path and in the distance, he was stunned to see the two kids from his neighborhood standing near an opening nearby. The kids were waving him on. Overwhelmed by the moment, Ryan finally understood. It was a metaphor. He stopped on the path and came to the realization *Sway* is more than a word but a living metaphor and or reminder.

Ryan said to himself as he looked at the swaying trees, "You always have our back, don't you? *Sway* is our symbol of faith. It's our reminder. You are with us no matter what ails us. We just have to keep the faith and simply let it be. We have to simply let it *Sway*."

He once again looked at the kids waving to him near the opening. He smiled and continued to walk the remainder of the path toward them. The closer he walked, the more the *sway* of the trees waved, and his heart pumped with enthusiastic anticipation.

Every step closer to the opening filled him with a jubilance he hadn't experienced in years. The sensation within his body was indescribable but incredibly pleasing. The further he walked, the more relaxed, comfortable, and youthfully excited he felt.

As he made it to the kids near the opening, he looked at them and said, "You guys have been pretty tough to chase down, you know that?"

The kids looked up at him and smiled as one of them said, "They are waiting for you."

Ryan looked at them and said, "They? Who's they?"

The kids point to the opening within the path. Confused but excited Ryan, looked at the unique portal opening and walked in. As soon as he walked through, he was hit with a warm rush of air, which whisked over his entire body. It was warmer and more pleasing than the path prior as he looked up and beyond saw a vast landscape and rolling hills filled with a sea of people in a tropical-valley setting.

As he walked into the valley he couldn't help but notice many of the people within the valley waited patiently for their turn to get in a line. The uniqueness and the immediate realization Ryan had was the majority of the people had clear and visible ailments. He saw people with paralysis, severed limbs; some were coughing due to sickness, and some even have scars on their face.

As far as the eyes could see, the valley was filled with people battling their own personal issues and ailments. Ryan stopped and tried to absorb the surroundings and was perplexed until he focused more on the line of people and where it was headed.

Curious, he made his way down the valley where the line had formed. He started to follow it into the basin. As he walked the line, it was as if he was walking through a sea of discontent. Everyone in the line was clearly afflicted with something that had challenged them in some form or fashion. Whether it was physical or mental, everyone in the line had pain they were carrying.

The more he walked the line, the more overwhelming it became for him until he saw in the distance where they were headed. Unsure of what he was looking at, he increased his pace of walking. His increase in step transitioned into a slight jog until finally an all-out sprint to reach the front of the line.

As he made it toward the front, it was evident the people were all lined up to walk through one of the most beautiful waterfalls he had ever lain his eyes upon. He stopped in his tracks in complete awe at the sight that was in front of him. The falls were surrounded by a tropical paradise unlike anything he ever imagined. It also led into an arch-like opening into another paradise his eyes had trouble viewing. The land beyond was so beautiful and offered an immediate sensation of comfort to him as he gazed into the beautiful rainbow-lit opening.

The people within the line were actually walking up and into the gentle flowing waters, which fell from above. As they walked through the waterfall, Ryan was dumbfounded as he watched each and every one of their ailments washed away. He could not believe his eyes as he saw a man with paralysis rolling his wheelchair into the water and amazingly come walking out from the other side and ultimately into the arch-like opening. He watched as the people with the severed limbs did the same and came out completely intact with all their limbs healed.

It would go on to happen to everyone in the line. No matter what their ailment was, the healing waters from the falls revived and cured their ailment. From cancer, to paralysis, to mental distress, it didn't matter. The waters from above provided the cleansing they had all sought.

Ryan could not believe what he had witnessed when finally, he watched as a man with a brutal scar on his face walk through the healing waters; and within seconds, the scar washed off his face only to reveal a clean and refreshed complexion. "Oh my god," he said as he watched them, one after one, repeat the process and then walk into the land beyond the arch.

Enthusiastic, he rushed over to the line and said, "May I get in line?"

One of the people in the line looked up at Ryan and said, "You're going to have to ask him," as he pointed toward a man standing near the falls.

Ryan turned and saw Paraclete standing near the falls and said, "It's him." Enthusiastically, Ryan asked another person in the line, "Is he who I think he is?"

A man near him in the line said, "You know who he is. You always have."

Ryan turned back toward Paraclete and said, "Yeah, I think have." Excited, he rushed over to Paraclete. "God? You're Him, aren't you?"

Paraclete looked at Ryan, smiled, and said, "Well, I have been called other things as well. Does a title really matter?"

"Why didn't you tell me from the start?" Ryan said.

"I've never been one to boast. How are you feeling, my son?" Paraclete said.

"I don't think I ever felt better. I think I understand. I really do. You're going to be there for us no matter what, aren't you? Ryan said.

"I would never leave you," Paraclete said.

"*Sway*'s my symbol, right?" Ryan said.

"Every now and then, I need to send a reminder. *Sway* seems like a simple way to do it. Do you think you can help spread it?" Paraclete said.

"Spread it? What do you mean?" Ryan said.

"I always can use a voice to help to remind," Paraclete said.

"Remind? But what about here? Now! Can I get in line first?"

Paraclete turned and smiled at Ryan and said, "You most definitely will, my son, but not today."

Dejected, Ryan said, "What? Why not? I've done everything you've asked."

"You most certainly have, and you have the gift to do a little more. Come, I'll explain," Paraclete said as he began to walk.

Ryan followed him and said, "What do you mean I have the gift to do more? I want to go through now."

Paraclete walked over to a boulder near the falls and sat down. "Come and sit," he said.

Ryan, somewhat dejected, walked over and sat on the large boulder next to him as the sea of people in the line continued to walk through the gentle falls and into the arched opening.

As Ryan watched them, he looked over to Paraclete and said, "I don't get it. Why them? Why can't I go through?"

Paraclete put his hand on his shoulder and said, "It's not your time. It's theirs."

Ryan sat back for a moment while thinking and said, "I suppose that's a good thing too, huh? I mean, that would mean I still get to see my family, right?"

"Of course you do, and even more," Paraclete said.

"Even more?" Ryan said.

"It's your time now, my son, to embrace your gifts and use them to inspire," Paraclete said.

"What do you mean by embrace my gifts? You can't be talking about this?" Ryan said as he pointed to his scar.

Paraclete looked at Ryan directly in his eyes and said, "My son, sometimes the weeds in your life are there for a reason. Sometimes they become a catalyst to build upon your faith while reminding others through inspiration."

Ryan looked at him and said, "*Sway*, right?"

Paraclete smiled and said, "*Sway*."

Ryan smiled and said, "It's our reminder, isn't it? A simple *sway* in the trees, a flag waiving in the wind, or even a breeze flowing through our clothes reminds us no matter what our ailment is or what our time of trouble may be, you're there."

Paraclete smiled and said, "So can you see why it's not your time? I could use a voice to help to remind."

"You want me to spread this message?" Ryan said.

"Can't think of anyone better. I mean, you helped your father and grandparents when you were just eighteen months old. Don't you think you should continue it on?"

Ryan thought for a moment and said, "And I guess the scar stays, right?"

"For now. Think of it as a great symbol and reason to tell your story. And you know what?" Paraclete said.

"What?" Ryan said.

"People want to listen. They want to be inspired. We just need more teaching it. Teach them to *Sway*, Ryan. Teach them to let it be. Teach them to let it *Sway*. And, always know, I have your back."

Ryan smiled as he looked back at the people walking through the waterfall. "We're supposed to embrace our pain, aren't we? The pain we endure are the weeds in our life. They're planted to help us grow, aren't they? If we can persevere through the weeds, then this is what awaits us, right?"

"You're a pretty smart kid," Paraclete said.

"Guess I had a pretty good teacher, huh?" Ryan said.

"Now it's your turn to become the teacher," Paraclete said.

Ryan smiled as he watched the people go through the archway and said, "So now what?"

Paraclete looked at him with a reassured smile and said, "It's your time."

CHAPTER 22

Home

In an instant, Ryan blacked out for a brief moment and awoke in a groggy state. He found himself lying face down in the middle of his backyard amongst the numerous weeds that surrounded him. He slowly pulled himself up and felt his face. It was still full of blood fragments from the thorns that protruded from the weeds earlier. His scar was more prevalent than ever. He looked around the yard while wiping the excess blood from his face and was perplexed for a brief second.

At that very moment a gentle breeze flowed through as he looked up and noticed the trees swaying in the wind. As he watched the branches *sway*, he simply laughed. In the background coming from the porch, Ryan heard, "Ryan, are you okay?"

Ryan turned and saw Norah standing on the porch watching him. Laughing, Ryan said, "Norah!

Oh my god, it's great to see you. I've never been better."

Confused, Norah walked off the porch and came up to him, "Are you okay? I've been trying to call you for hours. And apparently so has your new boss. He seems pretty pissed. What have you been doing and what did you do to your face?"

Ryan looked at his wife, smiled, and said, "I'm fine, really. Truthfully, I've never been better. And boy are you a sight for sore eyes. God, I missed you! And by the way, my boss, he can be as pissed as he wants cause you know what?"

"What?" Norah said.

"We're going back home. Stop your packing. We're staying up north," Ryan said.

Confused, Norah said, "Up north? What are you talking about?"

"Honey, I've been chasing the wrong thing for so many years. Our home is not here. This was just a brief stop in our journey. I think my time is done here and someone else needs to come in next," Ryan said.

"What are you talking about? What about the new job?" Norah said.

Ryan looked around the yard as the wind kicked up once more and trees swayed. "Oh, we will be all right. I have a new job. We all do."

He kissed Norah on the cheek and said, "Let's go in. We got a lot of work to do."

Confused, Norah looked up at the swaying trees and somehow had a sense of comfort in what she had just heard and said, "I'm not quite sure what you're talking about, but something tells me it will be okay. You're going have to fill me in, though." She stopped and looked around the yard. "And by the way, look at all these weeds in this yard. What a mess. You have got to get rid of these weeds."

Ryan looked around the yard at all the weeds and also saw the neighborhood kids playing next door. He laughed and said, "Yep, we'll deal with them. We're going to deal with them all. He looked at her and kissed her once more. "I love you so much. And boy do I have a story to tell you."

About the Author

John Cicero is the author of *Sway* and the *Rainbow's Shadow* series. He writes fictional, spiritually themed novels set in adventure settings—stories sprinkled with symbolism, suspense, and inspiration.

A current Cleveland Clinic executive, John has also previously worked in sports management for the NFL as a business development and marketing executive for the Cleveland Browns. John is a passionate weekend writer with a love for movies and books written for screen adaptation. His most important love is his wife, children, and growing family.